On the Other Side of the Glass

Bedside Books
An imprint of American Book Publishing
14435-C #155 Big Basin Way
Saratoga, CA 95070
http://www.americanbookpublishing.com
Printed in the United States of America on acid-free paper.

On the Other Side of the Glass

Designed by Jana Rade, design@american-book.com

ISBN-13: 978-1-58982-690-8
ISBN-10: 1-58982-690-6

Kari, Christi, On the Other Side of the Glass

Special Sales
These books are available at special discounts for bulk purchases. Special editions, in-cluding personalized covers, excerpts of existing books, and corporate imprints, can be created in large quantities for special needs. For more information, e-mail in-fo@american-book.com.

On the Other Side of the Glass

Christi Kari

~For Taylor, Maggie, and Casey~

Table of Contents

Introduction
The Holding Area

Before I begin this story, I should start by explaining a little about what happens to a person after they die.

In this particular fable, the first place a person lands after dying is a *holding area*. The *holding area* isn't a scary place; actually to be honest, it is a bit frightening to some, yet most will find it mystical and mysterious. People who don't go to Heaven land in this place seconds after they take their last breath on Earth. Persons from every walk of life, every nation, tribe, and village arrive by the millisecond through a long, brightly lit passageway that connects Earth with the afterlife.

To many of these souls, dying feels like being plucked from their everyday life on Earth and planted on another planet. One minute they were hiking, or walking, or driving, and the next minute they are passing through an unfamiliar pathway that leads to a strange place. To these unwitting souls, it is like experiencing an extension of their lives, but in another galaxy.

Oh, and did I mention the angelic escorts? Upon death, each person isn't left to face this unknown new way of life alone; an angel of death comforts each one with tender, consoling words, as well as gentle hugs, while escorting him or her through the intensely bright gangway. These angels of death aren't the frightening demon angels that movies portray them to be, but, instead, they are angels of mercy and tender loving care. Typically, these strong, supernatural beings lead the way to the unknowns of the afterworld, while the newly deceased souls take in the majesty of the galaxies they are trekking through.

Because the passageway isn't a long, dark tunnel, but, instead, a panoramic view of outer space, the deceased souls see all the unknowns of the universe. Believe me, it's one thing for a person to read about billions of brightly glistening stars, hundreds of billions of unfathomable galaxies, plus the brilliant sun, luminescent moon, and mysterious planets, but it is an entirely different thing to see them for oneself.

Naturally, these people are typically feeling overwhelmed and elated with what they are seeing, and curious about where they will go next. Most are feeling anxious when they reach the end of the cosmos, walk from Earth's passageway, around a corner, and into a large *holding area* resembling some kind of corridor. The merciful angel-men effortlessly carry older people and those who can't walk into the area and gingerly seat them on benches.

The majority of the dead souls' eyes are generally open wide, scouring the long, narrow area for something resembling home, but they only see large panes of glass above them and on each side, and strangers milling around, appearing lost and confused. Nothing seems familiar as each person begins to realize that he or she has left his or her family, homes, and lives behind.

Occasionally, people realize right away that they are dead, while others prefer denying the reality of such finality to their hopes and dreams. Unfortunately, no one is aware yet that they are not going to Heaven.

Since no one has experienced death before, unless they had a near-death experience in the past, which rarely occurs, everything they are seeing and experiencing is new and different. Some people cry in fear, while others try to take control of the situation. The macho men begin to size each other up to determine who will be leader of their section, and the bossy women begin shouting orders at the weaker beings.

The more frail ones in the section settle in, watching and enduring the chaos and noisiness of others with different personality types. Some are complainers, and others are whiners. There are the sniveling types, and, of course, there are those who loudly demand answers, although no one has any in the beginning.

As it is the way of God, no one gets to choose when he or she leaves Earth or how he or she dies; otherwise, the *holding area* would be sparsely populated. Even those who have fatal diseases, and know they are dying, still fear the unknown. They are the lucky few, though, who typically have time to get their affairs in order and make sure loved ones surrounded them when saying their final goodbyes.

There are those who welcome death as a way of escaping their unfortunate lives. Some of these souls are often distraught and confused when they open their eyes and see their guardian angel, especially if they have expected their lives to completely end upon their demise. These people aren't expecting to ever wake up again, so they are often angry when they realize life continues after their passing.

Still, there are others who are completely caught off guard by their premature catapult into the afterworld. They are usually disappointed at the things they still wanted to experience or accomplish on Earth.

Few die in the same manner either. There are people in the *holding area* dressed in hospital gowns. Some have incisions from where they died on the operating table. Some are missing limbs. And others have lost a lot of blood. There are firefighters, police officers, and people from the armed forces of numerous countries, still in uniform, who lost their lives on the job.

There are also those with less obvious signs of death, such as people who have died of strokes, heart attacks, high blood pressure, and diabetes. It is heartbreaking for some souls to look into the eyes of those who have lost the ravaging battle with cancer and AIDS. Their bodies are thin, and their faces are gaunt and pale for all of eternity.

There are also those who died of obvious blunt-force trauma inflicted by guns, knives, and vehicles. Blood flows or oozes from their gaping wounds; bruising and swelling make some unrecognizable. The scene is like seeing a zombie movie in person, though, thankfully, these zombies are not chasing the occupants of the *holding area* around, trying to eat them.

What is incredibly strange is that no one in the passageway or the *holding area* shows any signs of outward pain, considering the things that have happened to him or her. There should be cries from excruciating suffering; yet instead, people seem to care more about where they are rather than what happened to cause their untimely deaths.

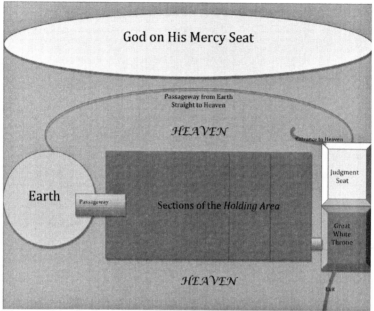

Diagram of the Corridor's Holding Area

To most of the souls, seeing all the blood is unsettling; however, there are no spooky ghosts, goblins, or eerie music in the *holding area* to incite fear amongst them. What is frightening to most of the inhabitants is not knowing what is coming next. For most of them, their emotions are keen to someone who is awaiting a tornado, earthquake, tsunami, or hurricane, but does not know when it will hit. People are feeling nervous; they are shaking and worrying about their futures.

To give you a better understanding of what the *holding area* looks like, it is a long, fairly narrow corridor that runs right down the middle of Heaven. The occupants can see the joys of Heaven taking place all around and above the *holding area*, although they will never set foot there. You might think it cruel of God, but you will read later on why it is set up this way.

The sides of the corridor are walls made of tall, thick, glass panes. The top is about a mile high and its covering is made of crystal-clear glass. The never-ending, brilliant lights of Heaven, or what God refers to as Zion, the Holy City, or the Kingdom later in the story, surrounds the corridor; thus, its constantly brilliant radiance lights the *holding area's* corridor.

Souls arrive in the *holding area* in second intervals according to earthly standards; thus, those who died at 10:00 a.m. are sectioned off from those who died at 10:01 a.m., 10:02 a.m., and so on. It doesn't matter what continent or time zone a person lives in; if they die at 10:00 a.m. or the following fifty-nine seconds thereafter, that's the section they end up in. Each section arrives in order, so it appears almost like a train with cars that connect, except clear partitions separate each section from one another, and there are no connecting pieces or wheels beneath them.

The sections are similar to escalators that float ever so gently, so the people inside won't be jolted or jostled about. In fact, most people don't even realize they are floating along, as they make their way from where they enter the *holding area* to the other end where judgment takes place.

This process occurs in different increments of time than what I mentioned earlier. Keep in mind that once people enter the *holding area*, its dimension is no longer structured according to the dimension of space and time that Earth is. Because this is the great beyond, a day is like a thousand years, and a thousand years is like a day. Gone are the anxieties of pushing, shoving, and rushing to one's next appointment or event.

Another interesting fact about the area is that it looks as if the people in it are around pre-teen and above in age, and they come in all sizes, nationalities, and beliefs. Each person's body is the same as it had been on Earth: heavy people are still heavy, blind people are still blind, twenty year olds are still twenty-something, and so on. They mill around in their assigned sections trying to figure out where they are and how they got there. Mumbling, grumbling, and whispering come from the area while people try to find others who speak the same language.

While people wait in the *holding area*, most feel immediately drawn to the glass sides of the enclosure, where they witness the unbelievable reality of Heaven. The panoramic view of the other side is intensely stimulating. It is more vast, more spectacular, and filled with more joy than most of the souls could have ever imagined it could be. People who wanted to believe in Heaven at one time, but chose to have nothing to do with anything *religious*, now admit the truth and shout about its glory to other naysayers. Even those who didn't believe in its existence now stand and watch in awe. They can hardly believe the truth of what their eyes are witnessing.

In the *holding area*, people are given occasion to reflect on their past lives on Earth, before the slow moving conveyor moves them on to the first stop of each section, which is the *room of files*. Once the conveyor comes to rest, hundreds of clear doors in the glass panes lift high for each individual to enter their personal *room of files*. A beautiful angel stands behind each door, waiting to greet the soul they are assigned to. Even though the people witnessed the angels of death upon their demise, most of them find it fascinating to stand before the large, supernatural creatures and look upon their holiness.

These beings are gentle, tenderhearted, muscular, and extremely keen to the nuances of humanity. It is their job to make sure each soul enters his or her own *room of files*, and then returns to their designated section in the *holding area*.

People often plead with the mystical angels for information about where they are, where their families are, and about where they are going; however, the ever-loving beings gently and tenderly lead them into their rooms in silence. It isn't their place to provide such information.

The visits of the people in the *room of files* occur simultaneously; yet some people's visits take longer than others do. Afterward, upon returning to their section, the dead souls again try to communicate with those of the same language, while introducing themselves to those they can and sharing stories of their earthly pasts.

Some remain silent while pondering their experiences in the *room of files*. Oftentimes, the reflection of their lives brings about disappointment, sadness, regret, and concern about their futures. Some people cry, while others are on their knees praying.

Once the celestial beings have safely returned all the souls to the *holding area*, that particular section then moves on to the *room of gifts*. Again, clear doors open in the glass to allow each soul to enter their own private overview of their lives. Some experiences are pleasant; these people have accepted and appropriated the vast majority of gifts, abilities, and talents granted to them. Other experiences aren't as pleasant; these people have been given the opportunity to gaze upon an unusually large amount of gifts intended for them, yet each present is left sitting on shelves unopened, unused, and often refused by the intended recipient.

The conveyor then moves on to the last stop, which is located at the end of the corridor—the *great white throne*. This is the room of judgment where each soul comes face to face with their Creator, Savior, and Holy Spirit. After entering the palatial *throne room*, souls do not return to the *holding area*. Each is given time to receive their judgment before they are directed to their forever residence.

Many of the souls realize how short their lives have been. They beg for second chances and do overs; yet, unfortunately, they learn that's not how the game of life is played.

Chapter 1
The Accident

Teresa Hernandez's body landed in the *holding area* on March 2 at 8:06 a.m., the same exact time that Anthony White and Victoria Valentine arrived. None of them knew each other, except that Teresa's eldest daughter was one of Victoria's adoring fans.

Teresa hadn't expected to die that day. She knew nothing about the afterlife; in fact, she was simply taking her daughters to school like any other day when a traffic accident took their lives. Consequently, she was extremely confused when she looked around and saw the faces of strangers in the *holding area* instead of her daughters, who had been inside the van with her moments earlier.

Anthony White didn't appear pleased about the interruption of his life either. He was a dark-skinned man, who seemed angry and intimidating, which was his way of making everyone in the *holding area* fear him. His large, muscular body was no match for most of the individuals around him, and he made sure they knew it by the look on his face. He had just come from prison where a fellow lifer, who had formed a homemade shank out of one of the cafeteria spoons, had stabbed him. Blood stained his shirt, forming a circular pattern the size of a basketball.

Victoria Valentine was the diva of the bunch. She strutted around the section as if she were the queen of Sheba, half expecting her fans to recognize her, yet at the same time acting as if the attention was troublesome and annoying. Her problem wasn't outwardly noticeable, but she was high as a kite, prancing around in her own little la la land.

But I'm getting ahead of myself. Let's back up and start at the beginning of the story. From the looks of things, it appears that Teresa's day would have started out as normal as any other if she had gotten up on time. Her alarm went off at its designated time of 6:30 a.m., but she had made a habit of hitting the snooze button two or three times every morning, and then paying the price when the girls were tardy for school and she was nearly late for work.

On this particular day, Teresa and her two daughters were running late again. It was already 7:30 a.m. and they should have been on the road by now. Angelica, the youngest, was hurrying to pour milk into her cereal bowl when she accidentally spilled it all over the dated, yellow, Formica countertop.

"No, Mija, I don't have time for this," Teresa shouted irritably at her youngest daughter, who stood motionless at the counter looking scared of the spilled milk. While grabbing a towel to clean up the mess, Teresa happened to glance out the kitchen window and saw Bella, (meaning beautiful in Spanish), the family's gray and white, indoors cat, stalking something only the cat could see in the backyard.

"Lupita," Teresa yelled to her older daughter, who was still in her room getting ready for school. "Hurry and get Bella into the house so we can leave for school."

"I can't, Mama, I'm not ready," Lupita shouted from her half-opened bedroom door down the hall from the kitchen.

"Ai yai yai," Teresa muttered under her breath, slamming the screen door on her way outside to retrieve the wayward cat.

Teresa had woken up on the wrong side of the bed and was feeling grouchy about her circumstances. It was difficult being a single mother. She has felt the weight of the world on her shoulders since she kicked Roberto out of the house. When she said her vows to him seventeen years earlier, she was committed to him for life. Unfortunately, Teresa learned later that she was no match to the seductive powers of his mistress—alcohol.

Roberto hadn't always been a drunk. The two met when she was a sophomore and he was a junior in high school. They ended up dating for three years. During that time, he was kind, chivalrous, and dedicated to her. They married soon after Teresa's graduation, and started their family right away. Roberto was a doting husband and loving father; thus, Teresa never regretted marrying him so young.

Their problems started when Roberto could no longer find work. Eight years after they married, the economic climate of Southern California changed and people had stopped building houses. Teresa's husband laid tile and marble in million-dollar homes on a regular basis, but, once the economy took a dive, he could only find rare odd jobs that barely paid the bills.

Roberto found it disconcerting and insulting that he was practically begging for work and being turned down left and right. He would have gladly retiled a bathroom or gutted the existing tile in a remodel, but no one even had jobs like that to offer. Roberto was too proud to get a job bagging groceries or flipping burgers, so the financial burdens of the household weighed heavily on Teresa's shoulders. Consequently, the man of the house felt degraded and usurped; therefore, he ended up turning to the bottle for his refuge…his drug of choice to numb himself from the feelings of failure.

When Roberto started drinking, everything at home changed. Teresa barely recognized the man she was married to. He began to neglect her and the girls, and, when she complained, he became violent with all of them. She hated him for being such a bully, and in her wildest dreams she would have never guessed her gentle giant had it in him to do such horrendous things to her and her baby girls.

But what happened one summer day five years later was the last straw. Teresa was cooking carne asada on the grill in the backyard, and the girls were dutifully placing trays of food, such as tortillas, rice, salsa, and lemonade, on the old, rotting, picnic table nearby. Hearing the squeaking of the side gate, both girls looked over their shoulders to see their overweight father entering the backyard, clearly intoxicated.

At first, he appeared to be a jovial drunk, waving his arms around and trying to swing dance with each of his beautiful daughters. But then he began demanding a kiss from both of them. Each of the girls eagerly gave their daddy a peck on the cheek when they were small, but too much had changed since those simple days. Angelica turned her little round face to avoid the stench of her father's nasty smelling, beer breath, causing Roberto to become enraged.

Teresa could hardly believe her eyes when she witnessed her husband grabbing their youngest and throwing her to the ground, then angrily kicking her in the ribs. Seeing Angel crying in pain and crawling away from her father in fear was more than she could handle. Mortified by her husband's behavior, Teresa knew something had to change, and it had to change now.

Teresa shouted, demanding that Roberto pack his things and leave the house at once; she could no longer risk putting the girls in danger, plus she didn't want them thinking abuse was a normal way of life.

Because they couldn't afford a divorce, Teresa and Roberto decided to separate indefinitely, to the chagrin of their hurting daughters. It was tough for the two girls seeing their family falling apart before their very eyes; yet, Angelica's bruised ribs were a reminder of what was necessary for their well-being.

Teresa secretly hoped her husband would get help and turn his life around. She dreamed of him coming back to his family one day, sober and remorseful, but, as the years passed, she gave up hope.

Life was hard for the single mother and her girls; she blamed Roberto for their circumstances and considered him a coward for leaving her alone to raise their daughters. Thankfully, Teresa had a job that paid the mortgage, but just barely. Naturally, she had a very strict budget to adhere to.

Two years after Roberto left the house and moved away, Teresa's mother, Juanita, moved in to help out with the girls. She helped Teresa with a few of the bills as well, and she took the girls to and from school, plus she prepared all of the family's meals.

Having her around took a lot of pressure off Teresa. The only problem she had with her mother was Juanita's religion. Teresa felt like her mother was constantly talking about God, the Bible, and the saving grace of Jesus. Teresa had heard it since she was a young girl—"God loves you…" "Jesus died for your sins…"—blah, blah, blah! She wasn't interested in hearing about any of that stuff then, and she wasn't interested now.

Juanita, whom the girls referred to as Nana, knew how her daughter felt about the subject, so she typically shared her beliefs with her granddaughters when Teresa wasn't home. She wanted to make sure the girls knew the loving-kindness of God, and that they were saved by the time she passed away.

Things were finally starting to mesh for the four of them until two years later when Teresa received a call at work that her mother hadn't picked up Angelica and Lupita from their respective schools. Teresa was certain something was terribly wrong; it was not like her mother to forget about her grand-children, so she left work and raced home.

Upon entering the small, dated house, she found her mother collapsed on the kitchen floor. Juanita had had a stroke, and broke her hip when she fell on the hard, Saltillo, tile floor. Teresa couldn't lift her mother without causing her a great deal of pain, so she called for an ambulance to take Juanita to the hospital. By the time it arrived, both girls had entered the home after walking the long distance from their schools, per orders from their mother.

Later that week, Teresa thought her mother was doing bet-ter. She was eating, having conversations with her grand-daughters, and talking about going home. Even the doctors' thought she might pull through, but instead, she succumbed to the devastating effects of pneumonia. Thankfully, Teresa, Angelica, and Lupita were by their Nana's side at the hospital when she passed away. It was a sad day for the Hernandez women.

Teresa struggled with the loss of her mother, and, to make matters worse, she had to take out a loan to cremate Juanita's body. Subsequently, the mounting debt exacerbated the grief she was already feeling. As time passed by, Teresa felt alone in the world. Sure, she had the girls, yet she felt somewhat like an orphan. Both her parents were now gone, she had severed all ties with her in-laws, and even at the age of thirty-five, she found she was feeling scared and lonely.

Depression from the mounting loneliness haunted Teresa, due to the fact she was especially vulnerable from mourning the death of her marriage. Even though she and Roberto hadn't officially divorced, she grieved the lost dreams they shared, the covenant each had promised to cherish and keep forever.

She wanted her knight in shining armor to come dashing in on his trusty steed and rescue her. Unfortunately, it was a fairytale that didn't come true. Teresa felt as if her life was on perpetual hold while navigating the waves of emotions she was dealing with.

When Teresa's mother was alive, she used to try to talk her daughter into forgiving Roberto and taking him back, but Teresa refused. It had already been five, long years and she wasn't letting him off the proverbial hook that easily. In fact, she wouldn't take him back for a million dollars, especially considering he made no effort to pay child support, or seek to spend any time with his own flesh and blood. *Was it really that difficult for him to call or stop by to visit the girls once in awhile? Why didn't he at least drop a card in the mail on their birthdays, or call at Christmas time?* she often wondered. *Did he ever think of them, or miss them at all?*

In Teresa's opinion, Roberto was off in his own little world, oblivious to his family's physical, emotional, and financial needs. She tried to move on and forget the abuse she endured at his hands, but, ultimately, her mind stored every offense, every slap, every punch, and every mean word in its computer storage.

Files were stored there reminding her of every visit to the emergency room, every forgotten birthday and anniversary, every broken promise, and every ounce of fear she and the girls endured at his hands. Teresa didn't even realize how the anger, bitterness, and resentment she felt for her husband was aging her, and making her irritable and lonely.

Pulling herself out of her reverie after cursing through the weed-filled backyard, Teresa finally caught Bella. Once the scruffy, old cat was safely indoors, Teresa hurried her daughters out of the house and into the hippy-style Volkswagen van. Seconds later, they were backing out of the cracked and eroding driveway and were on their way to school.

Teresa glanced into the rear-view mirror and saw the cute, little round face of Angelica, her studious daughter, catching up on her math homework in the driver's side back seat. Lupita, who was four years older than her baby sister and a strikingly attractive teenager, glanced over at her sibling and rolled her eyes. Instead of catching up on homework, though, she too was in the back of the van, texting a friend. Teresa proceeded to drive while she started making a mental list of the things she wanted to accomplish once she arrived at work...*First I'll disarm the alarm, then I'll make coffee for our guests*...The list went on and on.

She knew it was going to be an especially long day at the small, local, Mexican restaurant she worked at, considering they were having their annual state inspection. Teresa oversaw the bookkeeping, payroll, and receivables at the restaurant.

The owner of the eatery had asked her to meet with the inspector today, give him or her a tour of the establishment, and then sit down and go over the books. Arriving late would be unacceptable to Teresa. When she made a promise, she kept it, and she had promised her boss she could handle the inspection. Her heart sunk while picturing the disappointed look on her boss's face if she let him down by being late.

As a result, Teresa was hurrying through traffic, barely stopping at stop signs, when, without warning, the old, beige van they were riding in lunged, surged, and died right in the middle of a busy intersection. Dark gray smoke rose from the hood of the tattered old vehicle. *Ai Caramba! Not now you stupid van,* thought Teresa, as she banged her fist on the dashboard. *Angel can't be late again!* The principal of Angelica's school had threatened that one more truancy would result in suspension.

Now, Teresa was feeling especially guilty. If only she hadn't slept in, they wouldn't be running late for the third time that week. If only she had taken the van in to the mechanic when she noticed it was overheating, maybe it wouldn't have died.

She looked out the windshield for a gas station or auto repair shop so she could find someone to help her get the decrepit old van started again, or at least out of the way of oncoming traffic, but found no help. The concerned woman kept reminding herself of her appointment with the inspector and feeling more and more stressed out.

"Come on..." Teresa said desperately, while hunching over the steering wheel, turning the ignition key again and again, but the van still wouldn't start. She looked up and around again, and when she glanced out of her driver's side window, Teresa gasped when she saw a large, diesel truck plowing toward them. *Why wasn't he slowing down?* she wondered frantically. *Couldn't' he see them?* a voice inside her screamed hysterically. Sadly, what Teresa didn't know was that the driver of the diesel truck was texting and didn't see the stalled van in time.

Teresa wanted to move, but she couldn't. She wanted to yell and warn the girls, but everything was happening too quickly. She tried looking in the rear-view mirror to see her baby girls' faces one more time when, suddenly, there was a loud noise that sounded like a freight train slamming into metal.

Because her seat belt unsnapped, the impact threw Teresa's body around the front seat like a rag doll while the van rolled and skidded. She could hear the frightening sound of metal screeching across the concrete as the van slid down the street. Before she could feel the effects of the gruesome nightmare, everything went bleakly dark. There was no turning back the hands of time—no hugs, kisses, or goodbyes. Time stood still once the van came to a stop.

Chapter 2
A View of Heaven

The time was 8:06 a.m. according to earthly standards when Teresa opened her eyes after her accident. She was lying on her back on the concrete street, the bright sun shown in her face, or so she thought. She squinted, raised her right hand to shade her eyes, and tried to see through the light. Teresa then rubbed her eyes, trying to chase away the sparkling colors filling her vision. When she pulled her hand away, she saw through the bright rays ahead of her a large, masculine hand outstretched to her. *I must be seeing things!* she thought. *Giant hands don't just appear out of nowhere!*

Looking further, she watched as an image that reminded her of the angels she saw depicted in medieval paintings slowly emerged from the light. The angel wasn't a cute little fairy with wings that she always pictured in her head as a child when her mother told her about them, but instead a muscular looking warrior. She rubbed her eyes again, thinking she was surely hallucinating. He was magnificent to look at with toned skin, rippled muscles, and tender looking eyes that gazed at her with compassion and empathy.

"Come with me, Teresa," he said caringly, his hand still stretched out for her to take.

"How do you know my name?" she asked, while trustingly placing her hand in his.

He didn't answer.

"Wait, where are you taking me?" she asked, feeling him pull her up toward the light.

He only smiled reassuringly and repeated, "Follow me, Teresa."

Teresa wasn't the type of woman to just grab a handsome stranger's hand and follow him into the wild blue yonder, yet this situation was different. She felt different. The glorious being radiated a peace that beckoned her to follow him. She gripped his hand tighter as the two of them lifted off the ground and began to leave the scene of the accident. Soaring upward and flying with the angel was a stunning experience, one she had read about happening to other people in magazine and newspaper articles before, but never expected to go through herself.

Teresa found herself smiling in anticipation of what was to come, until she looked back at the scene of the accident and saw Lupita lying unconscious in the back of the van. *Why am I leaving her behind?* she questioned herself. *And where is Angelica?* Her eyes searched the scene that was slowly growing smaller below her for her other daughter, but the child was nowhere in sight.

Turning back around, Teresa began to ask questions again, but the angelic emissary tenderly and patiently touched her lip with his finger, quietly saying, "Shhh..." He then cautioned her to hold on tight while they made their way through the stratosphere. Teresa felt like she did when she was a little girl seeing glittering stars in the dark sky, yet now she was so close she could practically reach out and touch each one. Elation filled her when the sight of billowing clouds, the enormous sun and moon, planets, and mysterious galaxies came into view. She couldn't help but beam with delight that she was seeing things up close and personal that she had only seen through a telescope and in photographs before.

Once they arrived at their destination, the handsome warrior gently placed Teresa on some sort of heavenly conveyor belt. Seeing it reminded her of the ones she had used in many major airports in the past. Once she started to take a step, she nearly fell over. Her right leg hung at an odd unnatural angle that could barely sustain her weight. Seeing her situation, the sweet angel gently leaned her against his side, draped her left arm, which she also saw was broken in a number of places, over his shoulders, and helped her hobble down some sort of strange hallway.

Disoriented and confused, Teresa realized while running her good hand over her body that aside from a broken leg and arm, the wreck had bruised and cut her rather badly. She leaned against the accompanying being, wondering how in the world her limbs were still functioning when they were clearly broken. *I should be feeling the effects of pain, but I'm not*, she realized.

Teresa looked around in awe at the other enticingly beautiful angels who were also escorting people down the gangway. *And who are all these people?* she wondered. They were tall and short, Oriental, Mexican, Canadian, European—they represented cultures from every part of the world. Teresa noticed other people's wounds, broken bones, and ailments, yet they didn't appear to be in pain either.

What she didn't realize was that not having to suffer was the decree of a loving and merciful God. Even though the souls standing and walking in the same direction as her had rejected Him, He still loved each and every one of them immensely. Thus, He didn't want them hurting, or experiencing pain, at least until their judgment was over.

Once Teresa and the crowd of strangers came to the end of the portal, they rounded the corner and entered an area full of more people she didn't recognize; only faces of strangers stood around her. The entire ordeal was so confusing and scary. She tried to get her eyes to focus in on the faces in case she knew someone that she could go to for help and comfort. There had to be someone here who could help her and the girls…Wait, where were the girls?

Teresa remembered seeing Lupita lying in the crushed van and wondering where Angelica was at the time the angel arrived. Now, filled with motherly concern, she started to become frantic. Accustomed to being in control, and having answers, she needed to find someone who could tell her what happened to her daughters. Turning in circles the best she could, she scanned the crowd for her guardian angel but he had disappeared, leaving her all the more perplexed.

The worried mother started to yell her daughters' names, while her eyes darted across the noisy area in hopes of seeing her precious girls. Teresa didn't know it yet, but she was in the *holding area*. Surveying the dirty, gray-colored room filled with other loud, frantic people, she realized she was in some sort of clear-sided corridor in the middle of a large group of people that were separated on both ends by a small bit of open space—a sort of division. On the other side of this bit of space was another large group of people. Looking through the glass dividers up and down the corridor, Teresa could see more groups sectioned off from each other.

While trying to find someone in her section who showed signs of being in control, or who would at least possibly know how she could locate Angel and Lupita, she noticed that the people standing and sitting all around her looked ghastly. Some looked deathly ill, and others had serious injuries. Again, they weren't showing signs of pain, although they appeared as lost and broken as she was feeling. The majority of the deceased souls were staring out the glass sides of the corridor.

Curiously, Teresa moved through the crowd of people, and once she was next to the sprawling window, she too couldn't help but stop and stare at the splendor in front of her. *Ai yai yai! If Heaven exists,* she thought, *then I am definitely looking at it.* The majesty of it took her breath away. While brushing dark strands of shoulder-length hair from her eyes, she stood transfixed, observing the most enticing sight she had ever witnessed in her life, a sight beyond compare.

On the other side of the glass, a giant rainbow stretched higher and farther than she could see. Its colors sparkled and glistened as if covered in glitter. The blues and purples were more vibrant than she could ever describe. They reminded her of ripe, luscious blueberries and succulent grapes— Teresa's favorite fruits.

The oranges, greens, and yellows were so brilliant she could hardly take her eyes off them. It was like seeing her daughters' favorite dessert: lemon, lime, and orange sherbet displayed in a stunning archway. Looking at the calming brilliance, Teresa's day suddenly seemed less frantic and disturbing. She stood and stared, as if time had stopped. Not even thoughts of her daughters filled her mind now.

The rainbow served as a backdrop for people she didn't recognize. Thousands upon thousands of them were dancing, frolicking, and rejoicing. They seemed peaceful to Teresa while they milled about seemingly without a care in the world. Watching them, she noticed that each was clothed in a pure white robe, each body perfectly formed—none were old, maimed, or encumbered with pain or physical constraint.

Teresa wondered if she were watching some sort of esoteric film. She wanted to see more, as a way of escaping the drama of her own life and stepping into the curiously mysterious fantasy playing out before her eyes.

While her body relaxed, Teresa leaned her broken limbs against the glass pane and continued watching the grandeur on the other side. Without notice, her eyes widened in dismay when she saw a familiar sight; it was Angelica, her beautiful twelve-year-old daughter! Teresa was caught off guard. She tried lunging forward and yelling her daughter's name. She had stretched her good arm out toward Angel, when she plunged into the huge pane of glass. Looking high and low, she searched for an opening leading to the other side, but she could see no end or top to it.

As Teresa's body pressed up against the clear wall, she looked adoringly at her precious Angel and wondered how this could be. How could Angel be on the other side of the glass when she was with her in the van just minutes ago? Teresa began pounding on the thick shield of glass and screaming her daughter's name.

Angelica had just arrived in Heaven and was once again full of youth and zest. She was free from the pressures of her earthly life. The pre-teen was absolved from the tension presented by friends, teachers, and family, plus the high expectations she placed on herself. Angel would no longer struggle with being strong for her mother while watching her go through the stages of grief, plus the turmoil of depression.

Most importantly, she would no longer fear her father arriving at the house unexpectedly and pelting her and her family with vile words and blazing fists. Instead, she was home with the kind and adoring Daddy she had always longed for, and a new family that welcomed her with open arms.

Teresa, on the other hand, was desperate. She began to sob uncontrollably, through her continuous pounding on the impenetrable glass to get her daughter's attention. She screamed Angelica's name as loud as she could; then, all of a sudden, a new and even more shocking sight once again astonished her eyes. Teresa noticed her brother, Richard, walking toward Angelica amongst the crowd of people on the other side of the glass.

A horse riding accident had paralyzed him when he was eleven. He had lived until he was twenty-three and then tragically passed away from an asthma attack. But there he was, standing strong on his own with no need of a wheelchair. Teresa thought how handsome he looked—like a different person to her—less uptight and miserable.

Perplexed, Teresa shook her head, as if surely she was seeing things. *This can't be happening!* she thought. She wondered how in the world her brother could be standing there in front of her—alive and whole! His legs were now toned and strong; his body was perfect.

Teresa was further dumbstruck when she noticed her mother, Juanita, walking alongside Richard and lovingly placing her hand on his shoulder. Although Teresa wasn't privy to it, the two of them had been waiting at the gates of Heaven to greet Angelica. They were both smiling broadly when they rushed to welcome Angel with joyful hugs and kisses. Teresa couldn't remember a time when her mother looked so calm and cheerful. Somehow, she looked as beautiful as she had been when she was young and vivacious, very different from the last time Teresa saw her in the hospital when she had been ghastly pale, so near death's door.

Now, it looked like such a precious reunion was occurring, as the two loved ones held Angelica tightly. Teresa dearly wanted to be on the other side with her family. She reached down and pinched herself, just in case she was dreaming the whole thing. It was a childish thing to do she knew, but she was growing tense and uneasy with what was happening to her and her family.

"Angel, I'm over here," Teresa yelled again. "It's Mama! Bring Richard and Nana and come over here!" But the trio couldn't see her, couldn't hear her on their side of the glass. Talking and laughing with each other, they turned to walk away. With their backs to her, Teresa could only stare adoringly until Angel's long, black curls, containing the yellow ribbon she had placed there only hours earlier, were out of sight.

Tears welled up in the deceased mother's eyes again.

"What is going on? Where am I?" she cried, turning back around and lifting her eyes to her surroundings. Scoping the area, she truly saw for the first time what the corridor consisted of. She saw transparent glass panes all around her and even above her, and she felt herself moving ever so slowly through the corridor. Teresa wondered if she were in some sort of strange train, and, if so, where was it taking her?

Some of the people around her seemed calm, as if they weren't concerned at all with the outcome of the trip. Others, like her, needed to know the destination of the strange corridor. Seeing the sight of morbidity in her particular section of the *holding area* was repulsing, not to mention it smelled putrid.

One decaying man Teresa saw was missing an eyeball; blood dripped steadily down his face and onto his shoulders. A lady on the other side of her section looked as if she could have died during surgery. The hospital gown she was wearing exposed an incision in her abdomen. Teresa had always been squeamish around the sight of blood and guts, so she turned to avoid the sight of the stranger's decomposing intestines hanging from her, along with grizzly looking, white pus and oozing, green drainage.

Her disgust turned into a calm smile when she noticed people on the other side of the glass pruning gardens brimming with brightly colored flowers of every kind. There was every color of rose imaginable: reds, yellows, whites, and even colors she didn't recognize. She grinned when her favorite flower—daisies—caught her eye, then she saw Juanita's favorite—pale violet lilacs. *Oh, how I would love to smell one of those luscious clumps of sweet smelling flowers again,* Teresa thought.

She saw the innocent faces of children who were chasing each other around, while others were collecting fruit from numerous orchards and eating them. Purple, peach, red, and orange juices ran down their sweet looking chins. The scene was so innocent in her eyes—like one of Norman Rockwell's famous paintings. Teresa noticed that everyone on that side seemed to be free from worry or undue concern. Perplexed and bewildered, she leaned against the glass again and continued gazing upon the most serene, peaceful existence imaginable, while slowly making her way down the corridor surrounded by Heaven.

Chapter 3
The Voice

A flicker of light caught Teresa's peripheral vision. She glanced down and saw it reflecting from tiny shards of windshield glass on her top. She tried not to cut herself while brushing the glass pieces from her lacy, white blouse. Looking further down her body, she noticed rips in her black slacks and blood running down her shin. It wasn't a great deal of blood, so she didn't panic or faint at the sight of it.

Tracing the spilled blood down her leg to her feet, Teresa then noticed that she was standing atop an elegant cushion that looked like a thick, fluffy, white cloud. Shocked by the sight, she looked around to the people standing next to her to see if they too were standing on cloud-like cushions. Some were, while other people sat on padded benches similar to those she had seen in subways and trams. Each person was looking through the clear glass and admiring the brilliant lights, precious stones, and colors they had never seen before.

Teresa began staring, too, as her section of people moved further down the corridor. She began to make out the shapes of sprawling mansions far off in the distance. She had always dreamed of living in a castle—kind of like the exquisite, state-ly homes she was now gazing upon as her area moved closer. Teresa noticed the estates were unusual in that they weren't built from wood or bricks, but from granite, copper, silver, and gold.

Bright lights shimmered through each mansion's brilliantly colored, stained glass windows. The sight of these mansions brought to her mind a beautiful Catholic church near her house that she used to pass by when taking evening walks. The Church had windows with the same kind of majestic re-finement. The windows all along the side of the church she passed told the story of Jesus's life from birth to resurrection. Teresa couldn't see what the pictures in the mansions' stained glass were of, but the deep purples, blues, ambers, and reds that radiated from them were just as awe-inspiring.

The further they moved, the closer the mansions and oth-er buildings came into her view. Teresa was able to see that each estate was adorned with large, stunning jewels, such as rubies, sapphires, and emeralds. The embellishments were inlaid in the sides and fronts of the homes' architecture. As the light reflected from the precious stones, it sparkled, danced, and flickered. The sight reminded Teresa of when she used to see fairies in cartoons that waved their wands, causing fairy dust to scatter and reflect off the lights.

Her head tilted in satisfaction when she saw delicate flow-ered vines, such as white jasmine and violet morning glories, growing on the sides of a magnificent building that had come into full view. Not only were they pleasing to the eye, Teresa could imagine the sweet aromatic fragrance they produced.

Tall, statuesque fountains also adorned gardens set up in courtyards, as water trickled down from them and into large marble basins. Teresa could imagine the delicate sound the water made as she watched it drip in a rhythmic, gentle manner. Her eyes grew heavy because it reminded her of how the grandfather clock handed down to her from her mother sounded…tick tock, tick tock, tick tock.

She also saw rivers flowing alongside the never-ending gardens of Heaven; the one closest to her view wasn't like the murky rivers she grew up with. Instead, it was crystal clear and sparkled much like a gleaming diamond. The bottom wasn't slimy and green like the ones on Earth. It shimmered and glistened as gold nuggets shone through from the bottom of the riverbed. *I wish I could hear the tender sounds of the gentle waves,* Teresa thought dreamily.

Seeing the dazzling attraction, the people standing around and near Teresa clutched at the glass as if they would do anything to be on the other side, touching the pure gold and splashing in the cool water. Others screamed and yelled for their loved ones to notice them. They waved and called out in different languages, but those on the other side didn't respond.

"Where am I?" a very confused and barely coherent Teresa repeated. "Somebody answer me!" she shouted, looking around for whomever was in charge.

A gentle Voice that seemed to come out of nowhere answered, saying, "You are gazing upon Heaven, Teresa."

She was startled by the sound and even more confused. Her caramel brown eyes scoured the area to see where the sound was coming from. Looking around her, she noticed that the corridor had suddenly gone still. All around her, she saw lips moving as if people were having conversations, conversations she could not hear. Thinking about what the Voice had just said to her, Teresa realized that each person in the area must have been talking to his or her own invisible Voice.

At the reassuring tone of the Voice, and with the fact that someone was finally giving them answers, the tension in the *holding area* immediately began to subside. Of course, each person was initially shocked when the Voice began speaking to them, and Teresa could see they too were scanning the area for the whereabouts of the all-knowing Voice. She watched everyone in section 8:06 a.m. begin to settle down and converse with the Voice rather than with each other. Most had even stopped gazing upon the grandeur of Heaven beyond the glass. They seemed to prefer having explanations to their numerous unanswered questions instead.

Teresa was no different. What she was looking at through the glass looked like utopia to her, but Heaven? There was no way she could believe what she had just heard! She shook her head in denial at the thought of it and responded, "That can't be Heaven! This is all a dream." Then recalling that she didn't believe in Heaven, she wondered why she would dream about it.

"This is not a dream, Teresa. And I know you do not believe in Heaven," said the Voice calmly, "yet it exists. Your daughter, Angelica, shall live there with the Lord for eternity. She loved Him and considered Him her refuge. Praying to Him gave Angel courage and solace. After Roberto left, she clung to Him as her daddy. It wasn't easy for her to watch you mourn the death of your marriage. She loved you both and wanted her family together. She wanted Roberto to stop being so mean, so angry, so dependent on alcohol that he could not return home."

Teresa hung her head once she realized for the first time how the separation must have been extremely difficult for the girls. Life had been so challenging for her that getting through a single day seemed like a great accomplishment. In retrospect, she could see how her daughters might have felt neglected or even possibly emotionally abandoned by their mother. Teresa wished things had been different, too. She felt proud of the character her precious Angel displayed during such a troublesome time in her young life.

A flashback of a time when it seemed she and her daughter had practically switched roles entered her mind. She remembered sobbing on the couch one day because she needed money for groceries, when out of nowhere Angel wrapped her arms tightly around her like a mother would do for a child saying, "It's okay, Mama. God will take care of us. He promises to." Teresa immediately felt horrible recalling how she had yelled at Angel that day and told her she was living in a fantasyland, believing in such things.

"Angelica was a wise young girl though; she developed a close and special relationship with Abba," the Voice continued.

"Wait a minute, who is Abba?" Teresa asked, thinking about the '70's Swedish pop group with the same name.

"Daughter, Abba is your spiritual daddy. He is the one who gave up His only begotten son so that you and all of mankind could be rescued from eternal death."

Teresa had a disapproving look on her face and rolled her eyes, as she had seen her teenage daughter do so many times in the past.

The Voice continued, saying, "Angelica chose to believe Jesus was her Savior. She loved Him with all her heart, and it was her goal to live her life according to His wishes. Angel had wanted to make her decision public to her family and friends, so she had asked to be baptized when she was nine. Do you remember that?"

"Yes, I remember. I had nothing to do with that, though; that was all her Nana's doing," huffed Teresa. "That loca old woman used to tell me about gawwdd and Heaven 'til I was blue in the face!" she said in a sarcastic tone. "She used to spout off Bible verses too—all lies, that's what they were!" Teresa quickly let the serenity of the heavenly scene she had been gazing upon fade, becoming belligerent with the absurdity of what the Voice was telling her.

"Listen," the Voice said tenderly, "your mother was not crazy, nor was she lying to you. The Bible is true. Elohim, which is another name for our creator, loved you unconditionally. He watched over you every moment of your life. In fact, He cried when you cried, and He laughed when you laughed. That's how special you are to Him!"

"Oh, yeah, then why didn't he stop my father from drinking? Why didn't he stop my husband from hitting me? If Jesus is real, and he can perform miracles, then why didn't he stop that truck from hitting our van?" Teresa asked in a condescending tone.

"Teresa, God didn't create robots. He gave each human being the right to make his or her own decisions; He gave each of you free will. Your father's drinking saddened God. He's perfectly aware of the tears you shed each time your dad went into fits of rage. That's something your father was held accountable for. The same will be true of Roberto when he meets the Lord face to face one day. Each individual is accountable for his or her own choices, actions, and beliefs," the Voice said softly.

"Well, I'm sorry," Teresa said indignantly, "but that sounds like nonsense to me! I was an innocent child who was abused, and then an innocent victim of domestic violence. Why didn't your god swoop in and rescue me?"

"Actually, Teresa, He tried to. He wanted to be your rock, your comforter, and your defender, but your heart was cold to Him—you pushed Him away day after day, month after month, and year after year."

Teresa knew it was true, but she was fired up and wanted to fight.

"I realize now that you are telling me that my little girl is deceased, and she most definitely deserves to be in paradise, but my brother, Richard, wasn't perfect. He didn't believe in God either, and look at him now, he's over there!" she scoffed, pointing to the other side of the glass.

"No one is perfect aside from Christ, dear Teresa, but shortly after his accident, Richard prayed with your mother to receive Jesus into his heart. He repented of his sins, and, when he died, his reunion with God did not include a lecture and a list of sins a mile long. From God's vantage point, those sins are at the bottom of the ocean—never to be re-membered again."

Chapter 4
Dead Souls

After being in the *holding area* for what seemed like hours, Teresa noticed that the air around her had grown warm from all the body heat surrounding her, causing her to perspire. Turning to look at the other dead souls around her, she saw that some were sweating so badly that the stench of body odor had begun filling the air around them.

A gray-haired, overweight woman walked over and began to chat with Teresa. She bragged about her many accomplishments in life, including being a professor at an ivy league university, and having the ability to speak not only English, but Mandarin, German, and Italian, as well. After just a few minutes of talking her ear off, Teresa could tell that this woman who said her name was Maxine was the resident busybody. Apparently, she had gotten the scoop on most of the people waiting with her and Teresa in section 8:06 a.m. of the *holding area*.

"Dearie, do you see that young boy over there?" Maxine asked, pointing at a soaking wet Asian boy who looked like he was around sixteen years old.

"Yes, he looks frightened to me," Teresa commented.

"I found out he fell from his father's fishing boat and drowned off the seas of South China. He told me that he's worried because he can't find his father. He says he doesn't understand where he is, or why he has been separated from his father, who was in the boat the last time the boy saw him," Maxine said, staring at the desperate looking orphan. "Poor little fella! Drowning was always my biggest fear," she whispered.

Teresa was feeling sad for the young teen, too, when Maxine interrupted her thoughts with another piece of juicy gossip.

"See the man standing next to the teenager?" Before Teresa could answer, Maxine continued. "His name is Herb, he's from Germany. His clothes appear ripped and singed, because he was a pilot. He died by electrocution when his small plane sputtered and began to fall from the sky in a highly populated area. Apparently, he had a heart attack in midair and hit a power line; I doubt he even knew what hit him until he ended up here."

Herb was quite a sight. The plane crash left his body mangled and broken. Teresa was thankful he wasn't feeling the effects of the suffering he should have been feeling.

"That guy, Herb, gives me the creeps," said Maxine, cupping her hand to her mouth and whispering in Teresa's ear.

"Why?" she asked.

"He told me he used to be mixed up with a biker gang somewhat like the Hell's Angels, and he was also involved in lots of voodoo and what not."

Maxine didn't seem to skip a beat. Teresa's head was spinning when the old woman began pointing her bent finger toward the woman standing on the other side of Teresa.

"That's Bianca," she whispered. Teresa turned and noticed the smell of smoke on the exhausted looking woman who appeared to be Italian.

"That old lady's house caught on fire, and she died of smoke asphyxiation when she tried to retrieve her poodle, Chloe, from inside the smoke-filled home," she continued to whisper. "Poor little Chloe," Maxine said in a sad, pouty voice.

Poor little Chloe? questioned Teresa inwardly. *What about poor old Bianca?*

Teresa looked the woman up and down, only half-listening to her prattle on and on about this person and that, but found nothing that indicated her own cause of death. A part of her wondered if it would be appropriate to ask the obnoxious woman how she had died.

Maxine saved her from making the decision when she leaned over and unexpectedly announced, "It looks like I'm the lucky one here." She nodded her head in a smug way that suggested that she was an authority on the subject of which types of deaths were lucky and which ones were not.

"Oh, really. How's that?" Teresa asked, clearly amused by what she thought was an outlandish statement.

"I died in my sleep," the woman replied with an air of superiority.

Teresa sighed, thinking about how nice that would have been. She then wondered what made the woman so lucky that she got to die that way. She became quickly annoyed, thinking, *I can't believe this! She's gloating about the way she died! She actually believes she's more special than the rest of us! Give me a break! If you're so special, why aren't you over there, Lady?* Teresa was looking at Heaven's grandeur, thankful the older woman couldn't hear her thoughts. Of course, she didn't have the courage to say what she was thinking out loud considering Maxine was twice her size.

Not wanting to hear anything further from the nosey woman, Teresa turned and began looking around at all of the people Maxine had pointed out to her. After a few minutes, Teresa noticed something about the people and mumbled the oddity under her breath. While her eyes surveyed the area again, she asked, "Maxine, have you noticed that some people are old and some are young—probably no older than fourteen or fifteen—but there are no children here? I wonder why there are no babies here either?"

Teresa turned around and noticed "Miss Snoopy" was gone. Apparently Maxine had stepped away to share her antics with some other unsuspecting soul.

Instead, the Voice answered her by saying, "Babies and children automatically go to Heaven."

Teresa, caught off guard and startled from the unexpected response, jumped slightly. "Oh, why is that?" she asked, directing her voice up toward the sound.

"The Lord has a special place in His heart for little ones. His grace extends to babies and children who are unable to know the true difference between right and wrong until they reach a certain age," the Voice informed her.

"Really? What age is that?" Teresa asked, crossing her arms apathetically over her chest.

"Each child matures at a different rate of speed, but maturity comes once they understand the choices they are making and how each decision has a consequence, either good or bad."

Teresa began to shake and became visibly upset. Her eyes were big and scouring the area for an exit door, or an angel to assist her back home.

"What about my other daughter, Lupita? She was still in the van when I left with the angel! Is she still alive? She's sixteen! I've got to warn her," Teresa cried out while trying to push through the crowd.

"Calm down, Teresa," the Voice instructed. "Lupita is lying safe and sound in a hospital bed as we speak. Trust me, she is being given a great opportunity to make a decision for, or against, Christ."

Teresa looked relieved for a few seconds because, after living with Juanita all those years, she knew what that meant. She then scrunched her nose and asked, "Do you mean if we're not *for* God, we are automatically against him?"

There was no reply. Although the room was filled with people conversing with the Voice, the silence was deafening to Teresa.

"See, that's why I never accepted him. Too many rules! Too many expectations…" she cursed under her breath, while trying to march over toward the glass again, one leg dragging behind her.

A wonderfully scented perfume Teresa recognized wafted through the air. She turned around in time to notice an attractive, young woman sauntering through her section of the *holding area*. The young woman tossed her auburn hair to the side and sauntered around with one hand on her hip, looking around as if she half expected everyone around her to suddenly bow down and kiss her feet, or at the very least ask for her autograph.

"Oh, my God, that's Victoria Valentine!" Teresa gushed to no one in particular. Victoria was a famous singer, dancer, and actress. Everyone knew her songs and everyone rushed to see her movies. In fact, she had received an award that year as "artist of the year" for her riveting role in a biography on the life of Eleanor Roosevelt.

"I know you," Teresa exclaimed, pushing her way through the crowd of people slowly gathering around the actress to get next to the famous star. Small bits of cloud rose up into the air and disappeared at her feet as Teresa drug herself over to stand next to the starlet.

"You're Victoria Valentine. My sixteen-year-old daughter, Lupita, is your number one fan! What are you doing here? From what I've read in the tabloids, you've got more money than God. Couldn't you buy your way out of this place?" Teresa inquired jokingly.

The actress was taken aback by the stranger's outburst. She looked around in disgust, and then the individuals on the other side of the glass caught her attention. She moved closer to the oversized pane of glass and stared for a long time, then asked Teresa, "They look so perfect over there. Is this a spa?"

Without waiting for a reply, Victoria sat down on one of the empty benches, crossed her attractive legs, and demanded, "I'd like to order a face lift." She then snapped her fingers and requested, "Can someone bring me some of those delicious-looking grapes." She pointed to the other side of the glass where a bowl of grapes sat on a long table lined with other fruits.

No one answered.

Victoria looked around with a very smug look on her face, and then ordered, "Excuse me; I'd like to speak to the manager." As she said this, she shooed Teresa away with her fingers.

Clearly hurt and disappointed, Teresa limped out of the young woman's view and back over to a bench located next to the glass.

The Voice answered Victoria by gently saying, "Did you call?"

Victoria was so used to people catering to her that she didn't even look around to see the origin of the sound.

"Do you know who I am?" Victoria asked in a smug tone.

"Yes, indeed," the Voice answered kindly. "You are Vickie Ann Songtrot from Madison, Wisconsin, USA."

Sitting forward, Victoria huffed loudly and said, "No one calls me that!" This time she did glance over her shoulder to make sure nobody within listening distance heard her surname.

Irritated, Victoria shouted half under her breath, "Someone had better treat me the way I deserve to be treated or get me out of here! Otherwise, my fans will mob me as soon as they notice I'm here, just like that woman just did!"

She pointed over at Teresa, who quickly got to her feet and hobbled over to stand near her in hopes the woman was giving her a second chance at making friends. Before Victoria could continue, Teresa was by her side and asking the starlet what had happened to her.

"What do you mean what happened to me? Nothing happened to me. I'm fine."

"Actually," Teresa said, "we're not so fine...we're all dead."

"Not me," Victoria said smugly. "And if I am," she laughed haughtily, "like you said, I can always buy my way out of here."

"Now, somebody get me a pedicure, pronto!" Victoria ordered arrogantly.

Chapter 5
Turn Back!

Even though her daughter was no longer in view, Teresa sat back down and stared out the windows of the *holding area,* mesmerized by the sheer beauty of the Kingdom and its residents on the other side. She felt better knowing that Lupita had lived through the accident. This news helped her calm down and breathe easier. While slowly floating along on the smooth conveyor, she continued looking through the glass. Teresa couldn't help but smile at the sight of boys climbing tall oak trees and girls skipping rope.

She daydreamed of the happy days when Roberto lived at home. Teresa recalled the autumn day almost a decade earlier when he taught Lupita to ride her bike with no training wheels. She then smiled at the memory of how she had taught Angelica to hula-hoop and jump rope that same day. Her daughter's pigtails bounced up and down just like the young girls she was gazing upon now. It was a magical time the family relished for years thereafter.

As new scenes from the other side came into view, her thoughts shifted when for the first time she noticed that most of Heaven's adult inhabitants began raising their hands high in the air in gestures she did not understand. Many of the people dressed in pure white robes were kneeling, and each person's mouth was open and moving as if they were singing.

She turned her neck to the side and looked up to see what the fuss was all about and there in the sky she noticed what she had been missing all along. Teresa's mouth dropped open in dismay at the sight of something she could have never fathomed witnessing. She was astonished at the image she saw floating above the people in Heaven. The form looked like that of a man's torso, with a head, neck, and arms, as it hovered like a mass of white clouds in the brilliant, blue sky.

The figure was massive, it covered the whole span of the heavens. Teresa had never seen a face so gentle and adoring, or eyes that looked so compassionate and endearing, as He watched over the people below Him. The Being reminded Teresa of the father she had always longed for, as he looked lovingly upon His children—like a shepherd who refuses to take his eyes off of his flock.

Teresa was awe-struck, watching great bursts of lightning flashing forth, as if from a glittering diamond or from a shining ruby, from the Being that Teresa would soon learn was the Lord God Almighty. He was almost transparent, as iridescent rays of glimmering light shown through Him in all directions.

The sight of the Holy Deity was enticing, even magnetizing. Teresa couldn't take her gaze off the purity and glory of the Divinity. She longed to touch His face and be held by His strong, outstretched arms. Looking up at the immensity of the Being, her eyes moved down further and she noticed He was seated at a brilliantly, beautiful, golden throne which many people standing around her referred to as the *mercy seat*.

The throne that He sat upon up in the air above His loved ones was a magnificent looking, high-backed chair in gold, studded with every precious stone imaginable. Seven lighted lamps stood directly in front of the royal looking throne that looked holier than holy to Teresa, who could hardly take it all in.

In the heavens behind the throne was a swirling display of emerald rays mixing with amethyst flecks. Reflections of light caused a light show greater than any concert Teresa had ever attended.

Of course, she couldn't hear the sounds of music, but around and above God's sacred throne was a host of angels—seraphim and cherubim—singing praises and anthems in their massive heavenly choir. If Teresa could hear them, she would hear a song Juanita often hummed that went, "Holy, holy, holy is the Lord God Almighty—the One who was, and is, and is to come." Teresa could imagine the beautiful celestial sounds in her mind. She closed her eyes and visualized the sights and sounds her family was hearing on the other side of the glass.

Reopening her eyes, she saw in front of the throne a sea of crystal that reflected the gold, green, and purple from above it. It looked like an array of royal homage to Teresa. A shiny harp, as well as golden vials filled with incense, also reflected off the brilliantly clear floor. She couldn't smell the sweet aroma of frankincense and myrrh, but she could guess what it was after seeing the glowing embers that were producing the gray smoke that drifted upward.

Teresa was convinced the One on the throne was a king, but he didn't appear the type of king she had read about in history books or seen on television. He wasn't threatening or mistreating or ruling the people below Him with little care for their needs, fears, or dignity. He wasn't looking down on them as if they were peasants with no value or worth. Instead, He seemed compassionate and filled with mercy and love toward those He protected and obviously loved.

It's too bad she hadn't realized earlier that because the Lord reigned over his loved ones, never again would anything or anyone try to usurp His power and authority again, meaning evil was banned from His presence forevermore.

Could this actually be God? Teresa found herself wondering. *Could it be possible that He exists?* Only an omnipresent Being could stretch His arms and pierced hands throughout Heaven, as if He were balancing it all effortlessly, and then hold each and every heavenly believer in a fatherly embrace at the same time. Teresa remembered hearing something about God being like that in one of the church services Juanita dragged her to when she was a young girl.

She had to admit the glory of His holiness was enticing. She felt herself drawn to Him, and she yearned to experience His embrace for herself. For the first time since she was young, Teresa's heart softened; she felt as if she was in a cinema watching a good movie she never wanted to end. She felt mushy inside, like mashed potatoes. The sight was more splendid than even Hollywood could create.

Teresa began to think of the things on Earth that seemed beautiful to her: brilliantly colored flowers blooming, cascading waterfalls, orange and purple sunsets...but it all paled in comparison to the glory and majesty of what she was witnessing now. She had never experienced holiness like this before, or a father figure that made her feel safe, adored, and valued. Again, she yearned to jump through the glass and enter into His waiting arms.

Consequently, Teresa was feeling restless and frustrated that she had not been led to this Being she was drawn to or Angelica, Richard, or her mother yet. She was certain that someone had made a mistake, and the wait was starting to agitate her. As Teresa tried to make her way down the length of the corridor to find someone to sort things out, she startled upon hearing alarms going off and red lights flickering all around her.

A sad looking man with a bloody wrist bolted into section 8:06 a.m. of the *holding area* from the section behind it. Even though there were no connecting pieces, he evidently pushed a button somewhere that opened a clear doorway between the two sections and jumped through. Teresa and everyone in her area turned to see who it was and to see two angelic ministers of judgment race toward the raised glass doorway to stop the man in the light green, hospital gown.

Once Teresa was facing the man, he stopped in his tracks, looking disappointed and remorseful. "Oh, excuse me," he said to her. "I saw you from on the other side of that glass partition over there and I thought you were my wife."

A crowd of people gathered around the stranger, who was clearly lost and confused.

"Has anyone seen my wife, Sandy?" He looked from face to face asking the souls huddled around him. "I entered this place back there," he said, pointing back toward Earth's passageway.

"I have no idea where I am, but I thought I saw Sandy up here, so I crashed my way up to see her. I guess I wasn't supposed to do that because alarms went off and strange looking men started chasing me," he said, gawking around to see where the angels were now.

The frazzled, sandy-haired man then became quiet while looking up and around, almost as if he were hearing things.

"Did you hear that?" he directly asked Teresa. She was also looking up, wondering what he was looking for, and then she directed her attention to his question.

"No, what did you hear?" she asked the troubled stranger.

"A voice said to me, 'Joseph, your day has not come. You must return to Earth at once.' " He looked at her perplexed and continued. "You see, I'm just looking for my wife. Her name was Sandy, and she passed away last month from breast cancer. I just can't live without her. I mean, how am I supposed to take care of four young rambunctious boys when all I can think about is her?" he cried in desperation, as he placed his head gently on her shoulder.

Feeling her motherly instincts kick in, Teresa looked over to see that the two angelic intermediaries backed off and watched the visitor in her section from a distance. She told Joseph her name, then reached up and placed her hand on his arm, trying to calm the young man down.

"Don't worry, we'll help you find her," she offered comfortingly, patting his arm in a gentle maternal fashion.

Joseph relaxed a bit once he knew someone was listening to him. Raising his head from her shoulder and looking her in the eyes, he confessed, "Even though I know it's not right to leave our children behind, I tried committing suicide so I could be with my beloved Sandy again."

Teresa couldn't help but grimace in horror. He couldn't know that his actions hurt her heart, considering how much she yearned to be with her children. Joe, in turn, began to defend his actions.

"The darkness of depression and desperation left my mind wide open to hearing evil voices telling me to do it...to end it…to be rid of the grief by ending my life. I was vulnerable and weak, so I slashed my wrist and then ended up here." He looked at Teresa almost as if he was waiting for either her approval or disapproval, and then he quickly changed the subject. "Where is Sandy? Can I see her now?" he asked nervously.

She opened her mouth to tell the man he was asking the wrong person when she noticed from his body language that he was no longer looking at her, or waiting for a response. She was unable to hear the Voice talking to Joe, but Teresa could tell they were conversing, so she, along with the rest of the crowd, stepped back and watched from a short distance away.

The Voice repeated, "Joseph, your day has not come. Turn back! You are not God; therefore, you are not in the position to determine when your life should end. I understand things are hard for you right now, but you have work to do on Earth. People are counting on you to live out all the days planned for you."

Feeling ashamed, Joseph lowered his head. He was lost in thought to the point he didn't even realize the Voice he just heard was God's. He only had one thing on his mind; sighing heavily, the desperate man asked, "Can I just see my wife one more time? Can I hear her voice and touch her skin one more time?" he pleaded.

"Turn around and look through the glass, Joe," the Voice instructed tenderly. Teresa saw the young man turn around slowly, looking through the glass pane curiously.

Joseph didn't see the people in the crowd behind him wiping tears from their faces while watching the drama of the committed husband unfold. If he had, he would have noticed tears welling up in Teresa's eyes, too, and splashing down her cheeks. She didn't have to hear the whole dialogue to understand the romantic man's devotion to his wife. Teresa thought how she would have given anything to hear Roberto talk about her like that. It would have meant so much to her to be loved to that degree.

Peering through the oversized window, Joe's eyes locked onto the girl of his dreams standing on the other side of the glass in front of him. Teresa could tell by the look on Joe's face that the woman was like a delicate flower, bursting with radiance, to him. She saw tears of joy burst from within the widower as he reached for the translucent pane. She then noticed him standing transfixed, staring at his dark-haired beauty lovingly. His gorgeous bride was picking daisies with another woman.

Even though they just met, Joe motioned for Teresa to come over to the window. She hobbled next to him while he pointed to the other side.

"See, that's my precious Sandy," he said, pointing in his wife's direction, "and the lady she's with is her mother, Rebecca, who also died of cancer ten years ago. Sandy always told me how hard it was watching her mother fight that horrible disease—how could she have known at the time that she, too, would fight it later on in life?"

"Just look at them now," Joseph beamed, speaking to Teresa. They both turned to look back out the transparent glass as he continued. "My wife and my mother-in-law both struggled through a long, hard battle, yet look at them now! They are vibrant and healthy—no longer ravaged with the devastating effects of disease, chemotherapy, and hair loss. Instead, their bodies are young and attractive, their smiles carefree," he said joyfully. Teresa smiled while watching the two beauties stepping barefoot along the river's shore with ease.

"Sandy!" Joe shouted, while whimpering in relief at seeing her in her new body. Just seeing his lovely bride again seemed to fill the distraught man with contentment. His countenance changed once he saw his precious wife seemingly alive and well, and he appeared to relax, leaning against the glass, smiling with what seemed to be sincere, heartfelt joy.

Teresa then overhead Joe telling the Voice that Sandy had a limp caused by a childhood accident. She heard Joseph say that it seemed to him that his wife had always been self-conscious and insecure about it. Kids made fun of her in grade school, and, as she grew into an adult, she subconsciously considered herself unattractive, undesirable, and broken. With such a poor self-esteem, he said that Sandy seemed fragile and weak.

"Now look at her," he practically shouted in disbelief, gazing through the windows at his beautiful wife. "It's so good to see my lovely Sandy whole and flawless," he said to Teresa while smiling through his tears. "Seeing her free from the evil effects of cancer, while she enjoys her new-found freedoms, means the world to me," Joe added.

Without notice, the man jumped back, practically knocking into her when he caught a glimpse of the glorious face of God Almighty beaming from high above Sandy and Rebecca. Joe lifted his right palm to shield his eyes from the brilliance of the Lord's sacred luminescence.

"What is that?" he turned and asked Teresa in utter disbelief.

Before she could reply, the Voice began speaking to Joseph again. Teresa wished she could hear the conversation. If she had, she would have heard the Voice telling him, "I realize it's hard for you to entertain, yet what the Bible says of God creating Heaven and Earth is true. In six days He formed it all with His hands. He planned the days of each person's life at that time as well. Sandy's life is over, Joe, but yours is not."

Joseph responded by imploring. "I beg of you to let me on the other side for just a moment. I will return to Earth, I promise, but please let me dance with my wife one more time!" he asked, looking up in the direction the sound of the Voice was coming from.

By now, Teresa was sobbing as she stood next to this man who seemed like the epitome of a loving husband to her. Seeing him begging to dance with Sandy tore at Teresa's heart. It reminded her of the day she and Roberto danced at their wedding reception. Her new husband had whispered in her ear that evening saying that he would love her until the end of time. The memory brought about a deep sadness within her heart.

She and the others in the *holding area* didn't hear the Voice's tender response to Joe's request. "God is taking care of Sandy now, Joseph. You don't need to worry about where she is—she's very happy in Heaven."

Teresa did however notice that Joseph seemed to straighten up and look through the glass with his forehead scrunched. "Heaven? I thought that was a myth. I thought God was a fictional character in a book, like Zeus or Poseidon," he explained while standing and staring in disbelief. There was no denying what Joe was seeing was real. All of his previous beliefs seemed ludicrous to him now. He continued staring at the vastness of Almighty God in contemplation.

"God is very real, Joseph," the Voice pressed on. "He created the stars, the planets, the galaxies. He is not limited by time or space. He created every aspect of you as well. He knows your thoughts before you speak them. He is with you twenty-four hours a day, seven days a week, and He is interested in every detail of your life. Most importantly, He chooses to love you whether you return that love or not."

Joseph looked over at Teresa for an explanation, but she had only heard one end of the conversation, so she couldn't fill in the blanks for him.

It did appear to her that Joe was thinking hard about the experience and what he just learned. He had heard of God in the past, but, at the time, he needed more proof of the Lord's existence in order to trust Him. Now, as he watched God's outpouring of tender love, he remembered the many things he had learned when he attended vacation Bible school as a young boy at the local church in his community. Names such as Prince of Peace, Root of David, Jehovah, and Abba refreshed his memory.

It was obvious to Joseph that the God he had learned about earlier in life was definitely real and was even more adoring of each and every one of his children than Joe could have imagined. It appeared to him that one could not measure the magnitude of mercy and grace displayed by the Creator God with his or her earthly mind.

"That's God over there!" he exclaimed, smiling broadly and placing his hands on Teresa's shoulders as if he were shaking some sense into her.

She only stared at him as if he were a crazy person.

The Voice continued speaking to Joe. "Now that you've seen Him with your own eyes, will *you* believe? Will you go back and tell others about the glory and spectacular love of God? Will you raise your sons according to God's Word?"

This time Joe didn't take time to think about it. He blurted out, "Yes, I will! If God will allow me to live out my days, I will learn about Him, and I will tell others of His holiness.

I'm ready to go home, but I look forward to the day I will be reunited with my darling Sandy, and, best of all, my heavenly Father."

Then, for the first time in a month, Joe thought of his boys and how sad they must be now that he wasn't there with them. *How could I let them grow up without both parents?* he chastised himself.

Teresa saw the angels reappear and gently escort Joseph to the opening to the section behind her that would take him to the passageway that leads back to Earth. She waved at him when Joe glanced back to the window at the beauty he would one day come to know as Zion, and the Lord, His King, one last time, and then with obvious eagerness he walked the short distance to Earth's passageway, and stepped through the door to the other side.

Teresa continued standing next to the glass, looking upon the glory of Heaven and the One who hovered over the Kingdom on his royal throne. Lost in her thoughts, she wondered why it was so easy for Joe to believe in God when she still struggled.

Chapter 6
The Room of Files

The corridor containing the souls in section 8:06 a.m. had made its way down the tunnel running the length of Heaven and stopped. The group of people inside looked around curiously, wondering what the stop was all about. Some even asked the Voice to explain what was going on, but there was no reply. Seconds later, more than one hundred doors appeared out of nowhere in what had been the right side of the tall glass panes. When the doors lifted for people to enter, no one could see through them to the other side, but, when they closed, the souls could once again see through to Heaven.

The able-bodied inhabitants in the *holding area* helped those who were sitting or unable to move on their own to their feet, and each person made their way to a door. No one told them to do this, but each one of them instinctively knew they should rise to go somewhere. Each noticed the doors were labeled *room of files*, and standing in the doorway was a glorious angel waiting to escort each person from the *holding area*. Teresa and the others stared at the purity and beauty of the angels—such beings they had never laid eyes on before until their deaths and subsequent trek through outer space. People were awe-struck once again at the dazzling display of holiness set before them.

Each soul followed a mighty supernatural being through his or her open door. Anthony White glanced over at Teresa as he made his way to his awaiting angel. He noticed Teresa leaning on her angel-man, dragging her leg behind her, while the angel escorted the attentive looking woman to her very own private *room of files*.

Before he passed the threshold into his own room, he thought about his particular injuries. Reaching down, he used his right index finger to outline the bloodstains on his shirt covering his abdomen.

"Follow me," the accompanying celestial angel said compassionately. But Anthony stood still, his oversized feet unwilling to move. For the first time in a long while, Anthony was afraid.

"Get me out of here!" he yelled to the angel. The past few hours had given him cause to think about his life choices; thus, Anthony was not only feeling fearful, he was feeling frantic.

In a kind and loving manner, the gigantic angel-man gave Anthony a warm look. The angel's eyes appeared to be saying, "You will be okay."

Something about the glowing face made this large, fearful man relax, and allow the supernatural being to gingerly pick him up under his armpits and escort him through the large, arched, iron doorway.

Entering the room, Anthony gasped in disbelief when his eyes scoured the *room of files*. The room reminded him of a large warehouse without windows. It wasn't dark though; in fact, it appeared brightly lit by the glass high above that shone through to the ecstasies of Heaven.

Hundreds of multicolored filing cabinets covered the outer walls of the enormous room. Each stack of cabinets lined against the walls of the large, neatly organized area was color-coded.

"What am I supposed to do here?" he asked his escort inquisitively.

Anthony looked back toward the door and noticed that while he had been scanning the area, the male angel had disappeared, leaving him alone in the sterile room. The answer came over a speaker system. He glanced over and saw an intercom placed above the door through which he had entered.

The same Voice he had heard in the *holding area* spoke clearly and concisely, while the sounds seemed to bounce off the metal of the cabinets, causing an echo-effect in the large room. Anthony heard instructions to open each drawer of the cabinets and read the contents. The cabinets stretched from the floor to as high as he could reach, and were seemingly endless in either direction.

Where do I start? He thought, and then approached one of the tall cabinets. On it he saw a sign that read, *The Life of Anthony White*. Looking up and down the rows, he saw that each of the cabinets had a sign with the same words written on them. He couldn't believe his short life could contain such a magnitude of records. Looking further, he noticed the colors of the cabinets reflected the years of his life. Year one included dozens of orange filing cabinets. Year two's cabinets were all blue, year three's were all green, and so on.

Exploring further, he saw that each cabinet had a number of drawers with labels on them. Anthony noticed that the one in front of him read, *Friends*, so he slowly opened it. Because he had learned early on in life to be leery of his surroundings, he carefully peeked into the contents, half-afraid something would pop out and scare him. Instead, inside were many files, each with a name on it. He was shocked to see how many names he found; each was someone he had known during his lifetime.

Curious, he read another drawer's heading: *People Who Loved Me*. Again, he slowly pulled it out, leaning over to peer inside. The contents included names of relatives and even people he knew from childhood, kids from kindergarten, elementary school, and so on. Anthony was amazed at how many people he had forgotten about. Learning that they cared for him and loved him was humbling to the hostile giant. He stood and pondered the experiences from long ago before moving on. Good and bad memories flooded his mind like an ongoing slideshow.

Some of the names of people who loved him especially made him smile, such as Grandpa Henry and Grandma Evelyn. He remembered visiting them when he was a small child and eating cinnamon candies and snickerdoodle cookies until his stomach ached.

Other names made him wince with regret, such as friends he had let down or hurt. He read the names of Seana, Mandie, and Ylia—girls he had dated—and good friends he had known since childhood such as Mike, Jeff, and Rick—guys he had used to get the things he wanted—and even his ex-wife's name, Kathleen. It was hard for Anthony to accept the reality that each of the people named had once extended love and friendship to him, but, instead of accepting it, he pushed them away.

The cabinet below that one read, *People I Have Hurt*. Anthony didn't want to open it and experience the sadness he instinctively knew was coming. As if some unknown Being sensed his reluctance, the cabinet door magically burst open. Names he recognized stood in a line, their tabs sticking accusingly out from multicolored folders, each file a reminder of Anthony's remorse.

The first name was Josh Julian, a boy he picked on for no good reason in second grade. Then there was Kristen Hopper, a girl he made fun of in high school because of her bright, orange-reddish hair. His parents' names were there, his siblings', too. Anthony tried to slam the drawer shut, but curiously it wouldn't budge.

Going through the enormous amount of cabinets was exhausting. Anthony hadn't experienced such a multitude of deep emotions in a very long time. He knew now that owning his life choices included consequences he had run from for many years. Down deep inside he knew they would catch up with him one day, and, apparently, that day had come.

After he had poured through nearly three-quarters of the cabinets, Anthony stopped and stood in the middle of the area. Raising his arms and face almost as if he were looking up at Heaven, he exclaimed, "How could I have been so stupid? People cared for me, and I lied to them…I stole from them. I sold drugs to young kids, and I laughed when they got high…I actually thought it was funny. What was I thinking? People trusted me, and I jumped them just to impress my homies. I lost my marriage—my sweet and loving Kathleen—because I put my boys before my wife!"

Tears gushed down his cheeks while Anthony walked over, leaned against one of the brown cabinets, and sobbed. He realized for the first time how short life was, and that good people had been in his life for a reason. Anthony was astounded by how self-focused, arrogant, and reckless he had been with his choices.

"Can I please have a second chance at life?" he shouted up toward the direction of the Voice. Anthony wailed in anguish while looking around the lifeless, silent room. "Please let me go back and try again," he begged, pounding his fist gently on the front of the file cabinet.

The loving Voice came over the intercom, saying, "Anthony, there are no do-overs in life. God gave you every opportunity to turn your life around. He sent people to tell you about Him, and He gave you many opportunities to accept Him. He gave you many, many, second chances."

Anthony closed his eyes in remorse and then looked at the file marked, *People Who Tried to Help Me*.

The large man reluctantly opened the file drawer and immediately recognized some of the names: Mrs. Hockersmith, his high-school guidance counselor; Mr. Ostmeyer, his junior high football coach; his in-laws; his childhood pastor...the names went on and on.

"Why didn't I listen to them?" Anthony mumbled humbly.

"God had big plans for you that you simply wanted nothing to do with, Anthony. Even so, if you had been the only person on Earth, He still would have sent His only begotten Son, Jesus, to die for your sins. Christ paid the ransom for your sins so you wouldn't have to.

"When you turned your back on Him, He didn't force you to love Him. All He wanted was your acknowledgement and reciprocation of love. When you called him dirty names and said He didn't exist, He didn't strike you down. When you tattooed Satan's name across your shoulder blades, He still waited for you with open arms," the Voice said sensitively.

Anthony's head hung low; he realized what he was hearing was the truth. "I guess I'm here because he got tired of waiting for me."

"Actually," the Voice continued, "each person is given a certain amount of days on Earth, and your last day was today." Anthony felt the sting of tears in his eyes, as regret began to suffocate his heart. He began to breathe hard and fast. His chest began to tighten, and he felt like he was about to hyperventilate. Terrified, he started searching for an exit door.

While looking around, he happened to recognize titles on some of the remaining file cabinets that read: *People I Refused to Forgive, Addictions that Held My Attention, Idols in my Life…*

"Okay, I admit it! I'm guilty!" he screeched in sheer anguish. Sobs racked his body, as he realized he had wasted so many opportunities to turn his life around.

The *room of files* had been an eye-opening experience to see the kind of life God had intended for him. In reality, he saw that God had planned to pluck him from his harsh living conditions as a young boy in the streets of Detroit, and head him in the direction of living a clean-cut, wholesome life, where he could give back to his community.

Instead, Anthony had chosen a different path. His parents had tried over and over to remove him from the life of crime he preferred at a young age. They wanted him out of Michigan and living with his grandparents in Georgia, yet he continually ran away from them to live with his uncle in the heart of the city. His uncle had been a well-known drug dealer—a user and all-around bad guy. Of course, the unscrupulous man was more than eager to use the unsuspecting child as a mule to traffic his wares.

It didn't take long before Anthony was using drugs and selling them on the streets. The news of his actions broke his parents' hearts, knowing they had tried in vain to save their son from a life of addiction and abuse.

Anthony quickly made a name for himself on the streets as he grew into adulthood. The police knew him, and prosecutors knew him, yet he was unrecognizable to his loving parents and concerned family members.

The problem was Anthony had always bought into being self-sufficient. He wouldn't allow anyone to take care of him. When it came to God, he didn't believe he needed someone to save him—he was determined to save himself. Because of the gang environment he lived within, betrayal ran in circles. Thus, Anthony became his own god—the one and only being he trusted the most.

As he stood there reflecting upon his life, tears continued streaming down his face. It didn't take a rocket scientist to see the fool he had been. *Why didn't I listen to my parents? Why did I have to be so bullheaded? Why did I want to be part of the criminal element, instead of the person I had the potential to be?* he asked himself.

Now it was too late. Too late to save his marriage...too late to dismantle the gang he had formed...too late to apologize to the parents of the young girl he had brutally murdered...and too late to go back and tell others the reality of a loving God of second and third chances.

Anthony hung his head and placed his wrists together behind himself as he had done countless times in courtrooms when security guards escorted him to jail. Yet nothing happened; the large room of files remained silent. He was all alone in the oversized area. No attorney rushed forward to defend him. His ex-wife didn't run to bail him out. He just stood there alone and broken, waiting for his sentence.

Chapter 7
The Book of Life

Joseph, the man who tried committing suicide, was back home on Earth, as his wife, Sandy, and her earthly mother, Rebecca, smiled at each other while walking through one of the many luscious, green gardens, arm-in-arm. Their relationship was not an extension of their earthly lives, but they still recognized each other; therefore, they were no longer mother and daughter, but, instead, sisters in Christ.

The people from section 8:06 a.m. were each in their *room of files* when the occupants of section 8:22 a.m. were making their way down the corridor. Each watched the joys of Heaven taking place on the other side of the glass. They watched Sandy reacting to the softness of the green, mossy grass tickling her toes. They saw her look down peaceably at the daisies in one hand, and then smell the red and yellow roses gathered in her other.

Each person in the *holding area* could imagine the sweet smell and touch of the elegant, velvety roses. Watching her lift them high in the air, several of the onlookers noticed that as she did this Sandy was mouthing words to someone hovering above her. Each person wondered what she was saying. If they had been on the other side of the glass, they would have heard her shouting praises to her God, Adonai: "Thank you, Lord God! You are so good!"

A multicolored butterfly fluttered by and a dark-haired boy standing near her chased it with a net. Rebecca ran after him, laughing, then tickling him when she caught him, as the youngster giggled.

"I'm running again, Sandy," she chuckled, looking back. "My new body will never fall ill again. I'll never stub my toe again. I'll never grow old, or fight devastating disease again!"

"So am I! Amen, Glory to God," Sandy shouted in return.

Both women were grateful to feel complete—it was as if they both had the energy of youngsters again. Being young at heart, each woman had all the time in the world to marvel over the ecstasies of their new heavenly residence.

Ding, ding, ding…both looked up in eager anticipation when hearing angelic hosts ringing the high-pitched bells of Zion to alert the believers that someone on Earth had been saved. Everyone stopped what he or she was doing and raised their hands high to the God who hovered above them on His *mercy seat*. The souls began rejoicing and dancing before the holy Lamb of God, Jesus, who sat on the right-hand side of the glorious God of Paradise.

A graceful, slender-tailed, white dove flew next to the throne. Its soft, drawn-out calls sounded like blissful laments, and its wing beats made sharp whistling sounds. Heaven's occupants looked up, admiring the peaceful resonances of the bird with outstretched wings.

Each of the Christian saints then grabbed hands and formed a line that snaked through the garden as they worshipped the Lord for providing salvation to Earth's inhabitants. They danced around and raised and lowered their arms in unison to the beautiful melodies of the ringing bells. The souls were excited that another person had been spared from the fires of Hell.

While the believers danced, they praised God that Satan, the ruler of the world, for now, hadn't been able to trick or persuade this human into following him down the path of destruction. A celebration broke out as each and every saint of Zion looked forward to spending eternity with the new believer, who turned out to be Dominic La'Mone.

While Teresa, Anthony, and Victoria were still in their respective *room of files*, those in section 8:22 a.m. continued watching through the glass. Although the clear pane kept them from hearing it, the pitch and tone of the bells ringing in Zion was perfectly harmonized and intricately tuned.

As the never-ending worship music continued, Sandy and Rebecca noticed that the gold, ornate, entrance gates were ajar. The two ladies headed in the direction of the attractive woman who was arriving through the gates of the Holy City. They didn't know her, but it was Dominic La'Mone's wife, Emma. She had just perished, and she was tickled pink once she saw the glory of Heaven's splendor spread out before her.

She had nearly missed this opportunity, and the relieved, joyous look on her face acknowledged that she was especially grateful that things hadn't turned out differently. Each and every soul in the *holding area* watched her, and wished they were in her shoes, while she met her father and other loved ones who had preceded her in death. They had no idea how easily her story could have ended up differently if she hadn't realized the truth in time.

As I mentioned, Emma was married to the man the saints of Heaven were ringing the bells about—Dominic La'Mone.

Let me tell you their story so you will see why Emma's life choices took a dramatic turn that landed her in Heaven.

Dominic La'Mone was a famous hockey player from Canada who had lived a double life far from thoughts of God. Upon being recruited to the NHL in America, he moved his family to the east coast to play for the New York Rangers. The La'Mones owned a large home in New York City, a summer home on the west coast, and they had many household servants. Dominic and his slender, attractive wife, Emma, drove luxurious vehicles, and their twin children attended a private school.

The La'Mone family relished the American way of life, and especially being in the limelight. Emma particularly enjoyed the paparazzi seeking her out. The thirty-two-year-old was quickly becoming a clothes conesour, so fashion designers sought her for advice on their upcoming lines. Emma enjoyed showing off her private collections, fancy shoes, and dazzling jewels.

Although it was unusual for her to be home, one day Emma found a stack of pornographic material hidden in the master bedroom closet. When she asked Dominic about them, he shrugged it off.

"All men look at 'girlie magazines,'" he retorted, annoyed that his wife would try to make him feel guilty about such a trivial guy thing.

Even though she was surprised at Dom's lackadaisical attitude, Emma didn't think much about it at first because he was right she admitted—a lot of men do keep such things hidden away. Then one day a porn site popped up while she was on his computer searching the Internet for new software programs that would make it easier for her to create her fashions.

Curious, Emma searched the *history* and found many pornographic sites and chat rooms. Seeing all those sites hurt and angered her. She felt disgusted and ashamed that she wasn't enough for her husband and planned to confront him when he returned home. Of course, upon his arrival, Dom accused Emma of overreacting when she practically bit his head off before he could get through the threshold of the elegant, arched, front door.

"It's no big deal, Em!" he reassured her.

"It is to me!" she yelled. "Why do you look at pictures of naked women when you have me? Every time you make a mental picture of one of them, you are rejecting the image of me, and replacing me in your heart and mind with them. How do you think that makes me feel?" Emma asked, glaring at Dominic. He only rolled his eyes, in a sign that said he thought Em was being overly dramatic. His dismissive attitude was one he used when he thought it was her time of the month.

"Dom, I can't compete with images of women who have had plastic surgery, enhancements, and digital touchups. It's like being in an unfair competition that I can't possibly win!" she cried. Visions of working out more, eating less, and buying sexier clothes filled her jumbled mind. Finally, out of sheer desperation, Em looked into her handsome groom's eyes and pleaded. "Do you want me to get a breast enhancement? Should I get a face lift?" she asked, feeling her face for wrinkles.

Dom appeared to be embarrassed at how Emma was reacting, so he tried changing the subject. "Emmie, come here and let daddy make you feel all better," said Dom, as his muscle-bound arms groped Em's buttocks and started moving upwards.

"Stop it, Dom!" Emma shouted, disgusted that he thought taking her to bed would shut her up. "You're such a jerk!" she shouted in annoyance while trying to break his strong hands free from her petite waist.

"Okay, Emmie," he shrugged, removing his hands from her and trying another approach. "Why don't you get dressed up and I'll take you to dinner so you can show off that fancy, diamond, tennis bracelet I just bought you."

Em absolutely hated it when Dom patronized her like that. *How could he be so nonchalant and cavalier about such a serious subject?* she wondered. She felt demoralized and defiled.

"I want you to get rid of all the magazines and inappropriate videos in this house!" she demanded loudly. "I want you to stop going to porn shops and strip shows. I want you to…"

"Honey, get over it!" Dom yelled at her in a voice so harsh and so full of venom she cringed away from him. Em hadn't heard him shout like that in a long time. She realized she must have hit a nerve with him, and she was afraid the children would hear, so she shushed him. Annoyed and unrepentant, the star athlete got the last word.

"Look how you live," he said, gesturing to their surroundings. "Just let me do my thing and you can have all this."

Emma, outraged and humiliated, began to cry. Knowing it was a childish thing to do, but wanting some time alone to lick her wounds, so to speak, she ran to the master bedroom and locked herself in. Throwing herself down on the satin duvet, Em cried into her pillow to muffle the sounds from her children, and lay there wondering how Dom would feel if she cheated on him like that. After several hours, the phone rang; a movie producer was calling to schedule an interview with her. Reality hit when Em realized her celebrity piggybacked her husband's fame.

The thought of losing it all was too much for Emma to bear, so she got up and dressed for dinner. Packing on makeup to cover her puffy eyes and blotchy face, she decided to keep quiet about the whole thing. After spending hours mulling over her situation, Em had convinced herself that Dom was right—she had made a fuss about nothing.

Things went back to normal, until a month later when one of Emma's arrogant "friends" called to gloat that the police had arrested Dominic on prostitution charges in California. Of course, Emma was mortified. She immediately turned on the television to one of the local sports news channels and saw that the media was having a frenzy over it.

She found out the full truth about her husband's secret sins from the broadcast; Dominic had an uncontrollable sexual addiction. He had succumbed to living out his fantasies with prostitutes when he was making commercials, or training, or attending business meetings in Los Angeles.

Not only was she shocked; Emma was enraged and embarrassed that her Prince Charming had yielded to such selfish pleasures. She especially felt shame over how people would view her now. *How could Dom do this to me?* she cried. Emma felt stupid and pathetic when she noticed the household servants glancing at her with looks of pity.

For weeks, she tried shielding the twins from the tabloids, newspapers, and news shows. In her mind, they didn't deserve to have their lives disrupted by Dominic's poor choices. She didn't want her twins', Simon and Alexandra, reputation being dragged through the mud either.

As time marched on, Emma sank into a depression. Her

mind constantly conjured images of her husband with other women. Emma pictured them in bed together…in the shower together. It was enough to drive her stark raving mad. She wasn't herself; even helping the kids and being there for them was a chore. The once vibrant up-and-coming celebrity barely had the energy to help herself. Consequently, Em ended up spending hours in bed, wondering how many women her husband had been with. Questions about how many times he had lied to her face filled her thoughts, as well.

Brokenhearted seemed like an understatement when describing Emma La'Mone those first few weeks after her husband was arrested. She couldn't help but feel alone; there was no one she could talk to who wouldn't leak her feelings to the media. Em was too embarrassed to call her mother, or her girlfriends. She had no one with whom she could trust with her pain. Dominic had always been her god, her rock, and her fortress. Now she felt abandoned, betrayed, and alone, while dealing with the ugly effects of infidelity.

Over time, Em was shocked to learn via Internet chat rooms and support groups just how many other families were ripped apart due to the insidious nature of pornography and sexual addiction. It was sad that she and her family were just another statistic in the percentage of broken families in America. Since she considered it all Dom's fault, Em decided she wanted nothing to do with her husband—no counseling sessions, no forgiveness, and no mercy. The sheer sight of him repulsed her.

Once everything was said and done, Dom's attorney made sure Dom didn't get too much jail time, but, because it was his second offense, which he and his agent had painstakingly managed to hide from Emma and the media, his coaches suspended him for the rest of the season, and said he wouldn't be returning the following October.

Also, Dom had been training with the American Olympic team; therefore, he lost his spot on the team, plus his endorsements. As a result, the La'Mones' bank accounts dwindled quickly. Debt collectors and creditors began calling at all hours of the day and night. Once Emma realized the surmounting debt they were in, she put her shame aside, took the kids, and returned to Canada to live with her mother.

Eventually the cars were repossessed, the second home was foreclosed upon, the servants were laid off, and Dominic was left alone in his mansion. He had lost everything…his good reputation, his successful career, all of his material possessions, and his family. While sitting on the cold, marble floor for what seemed like an hour, he wondered how it all began. He couldn't understand how simply looking at the naked images of women most men ogled over could explode into such an evil addiction.

He pondered his childhood, remembering how it felt when he found his first illicit magazine. It belonged to his father, and once he knew Dom was looking at it too, he seemed to approve. It was sort of their man-to-man secret.

As Dom grew older, he began to tire of the soft porn and craved more and more unhealthy habits, that eventually led to a full-blown addiction. Of course, he didn't realize what was happening, although he knew all along what he was doing was wrong; otherwise, he wouldn't have hidden it. Now his secret was out.

While sitting alone and thinking about it, Dom admitted to himself how he had secretly hoped Emma had violated the boundaries of their marriage, too, so he would feel vindicated. Thinking of how self-centered that thought was made him feel sick to his stomach. *How could I have been so selfish and narcissistic?* he wondered. After a while, it seemed as if his head was spinning from the shame and guilt flooding his mind.

Sitting alone in the mansion, he began to sob uncontrollably, his body racked with disgust and regret. Dominic wished he could turn back the hands of time.

"God, how could you do this to me?" he shouted, raising his eyes and his fist to the ceiling. "How could you let this happen?" he screamed, slumping to the ground, dropping his face in his hands, and beginning to cry.

Sitting on the cold floor, Dom looked up and surveyed the quiet, empty house. *This was the home we celebrated the twins' seventh birthday in*, he remembered. Looking over to the dark granite, kitchen counter, the buff father pictured Simon and Alexandra one year earlier blowing out colorful candles on their birthday cakes. Simon had picked up a pile of chocolate frosting and slathered it all over his sister's face, causing her to chase him all over the house, screaming that she would beat him up for that. Dom chuckled at the memory.

He then pictured the twins marveling at how beautiful their mother looked when they glanced up and watched her sauntering down the tall, arched staircase in the middle of the home. Dom had bought her a diamond necklace to celebrate their ten-year wedding anniversary. Once she reached the landing of the stairs, she gleefully twirled around for the family in the living room, while modeling a fabulous dress she had designed adorned with the stunning necklace.

Now the kitchen was empty…the stairway was lifeless. Not only was the living room empty of furniture, it was now devoid of life and exuberance…void of the family Dom adored, the family he took for granted.

Moving trucks arrived later that same afternoon to re-move the remaining rental furniture, and the bank officer came to retrieve the keys to the house from him. Dom stood outside for a long time just staring at the mansion, wondering how he had allowed this tragedy to occur.

Where are all of my fans now? Dom wondered resentfully. *Where are all the women who threw themselves at me?* He realized that his coaches and agents weren't even there for him. It was as if he had some type of horrible contagious disease that no one wanted to catch. Even so, he knew everything that had happened to him—his career and his family—was his fault. It seemed the loneliness was deafening while he was lost in his thoughts.

How could it be that Dominic La'Mone, the famous athlete, was now homeless? he wondered. As it began to snow, Dom looked up at the dark sky and shivered. Looking around the deserted neighborhood, he realized he had nowhere to go. Walking down the quiet street, he kicked angrily at snowdrifts, realiz-ing how badly he had let his family down. Not knowing where to go next, Dom started toward downtown and finally ended up in front of a homeless shelter. The building blocked the wind chill, and, if he stood just right, the wooden eave kept the freezing snow from falling on his shoulders.

Leaning against the exterior wall of the shelter, Dom cupped his hands together and warmed them with his breath. He was feeling grateful that he had become accustomed to cold weather while living in Canada. After an hour or so of standing alone watching people come and go out of the building, a big, burly man walked up and asked in a gruff voice, "You going in, Mister?"

Dominic pulled his stocking cap down over his eyes so the man wouldn't recognize him. He then tried to disguise his voice so the man wouldn't notice his French accent. "No, man, I don't want to take food or a cot from a woman or child."

"Okay, then why don't you come in for some hot coffee?" he said, gesturing to the door.

"Sure," Dominic replied humbly, entering the building. The large man, who said his name was Harold, escorted Dom inside and then introduced him to Jeremiah Jones, a dark-skinned man who looked as if he was in his fifties. After Harold introduced them, Jeremiah reached his hand up from his desk and shook Dom's while Harold exited the room.

"Hi, there. I'm Jeremiah, but you can call me Jerry," the director of the facility said while standing and pushing his glasses up to the bridge of his nose.

Jerry gestured for Dominic to sit down, and then he brought two cups of steaming coffee over from atop a small shelf next to his desk. He took his own seat while the two men began talking and sipping dark, black, hot coffee. Jerry seemed to be a God-fearing man who listened with compassion while Dominic began spilling his guts about what had happened to him. He shared about his family, his successful career, and subsequent rise to fame.

Dom couldn't hold the tears back as he told Jerry the details of what had transpired the previous couple months. Jerry was taken aback when he heard the hockey player say he couldn't believe a guy like himself could lose everything—especially due to such a minor offense such as pornography, (he purposely left the part about adultery out).

Jerry stopped the star athlete in his tracks, and said, "It looks like you've missed the point, Dom. There is an underlying issue that you need to discover and address. Your obsession with porn may have seemed innocent enough, but the secret sin morphed into a full-blown addiction, all because of the underlying issue."

"Underlying issue?" Dom asked, his brows furled in obvious confusion.

Jerry continued. "Our addictions take our focus off God." He then told Dom that in his case, living in a world of fantasy and lies gave the devil a foothold, or rather, the opportunity to create consequences that would trip him up and make him fall.

Dom looked at Jerry as if he were speaking a foreign language...*God? The devil? Give me a break*, he thought.

Harold, the big guy who had escorted Dom inside, interrupted the two men by telling Jerry that he needed help finding room for a family that had just shown up. Jerry left to show Harold where a few extra cots were located in storage.

When the director returned, he continued. "Actually, Dom, being homeless and destitute is probably the best thing that could ever happen to you."

"What?" Dominic shouted in anger. He knew it. This guy was a whack job—he didn't know what he was talking about. "How can you say such a horrible thing? You sit there and judge me, and then tell me you're happy this has happened to me?" Dominic had always thought men like Jerry were weaklings who used Christianity as a crutch.

He stood to leave, but Jerry reached out, grabbed his arm, and said, "Sit down, you need to let me finish." Dominic started to resist, but begrudgingly sat back down on the rickety stool.

"Dom, God didn't do this *to* you, *you* did this to yourself. Addictions are evil—actually, they are jealous. They want all of your focus and attention. If you try to break loose from them, they work hard to pull you back. God allowed you to hit rock bottom so that you would look up—up to Him—so you would take your eyes off yourself and your fantasies, and seek after Him for direction and purpose."

"Purpose?" Dom questioned. "Hockey was my purpose in life. Now, I have nothing!"

"Not true," said Jeremiah. "You have a family here on Earth. You have a loving Father in Heaven extending His hand of grace—the unearned and undeserved gift of forgiveness of every sin, even the ones He loathes. You have a choice to either resist Him, or surrender control of your life to the One who created you."

"Man, I'm a competitor. I don't surrender to anyone," Dominic said with indignation.

Again, Harold sheepishly entered Jerry's office, stating that he had run out of sheets and pillows. He had heard raised voices and what appeared to be arguing, so he was afraid to interrupt, but since it was the first snowfall of the season, many homeless people were entering the warm shelter. Once Jerry was behind his desk again after helping Harold, he spoke further with Dom.

"Look," Jerry continued, "the Bible says that one day every knee will bow and every tongue will confess the glory of the Lord. Do you want to submit voluntarily, or do you want to be sided with God's enemy?"

"Enemy? What are you talking about, man?"

"Dom, when you were playing hockey, your opponent was your enemy, right? Well, in this case, Satan is God's nemesis. His goal is to keep every soul from God that he can. He lures each of us with bait: money, pleasures, power, and lies. Once a person bites the proverbial hook, evil masters him or her, and darkness will prevail in the form of addictions, abuse, and abandonment." Jerry looked Dom in the eyes and asked,

"Does this sound at all familiar to you?"

Dominic looked away, evading the director's poignant question.

Jerry didn't skip a beat as he continued talking to the famous athlete. "The evil one is crafty and he can even make a person defend his own sinful actions."

Dom was distracted for a few seconds while trying to decide if he believed in the devil, and missed Jerry's last statement.

"What were you saying?" Dom asked, as he reverted his attention back to the kind and caring man.

"I said, once Satan has a person completely distracted and disillusioned, he drives the person to defend their own sinful actions. For instance, he seduced you into believing your lifestyle was normal; he had you so focused on fantasy that you lost touch with reality. His intention was to steal your joy, kill your marriage, and destroy any chance you had of having a relationship with Christ. He wanted you so low that soon you would even be considering killing yourself. He does this to people in order to snatch their souls from God. It's one of his craftiest tricks."

"Wow," Dom said. He knew that part was definitely true because he had been contemplating suicide himself. It would have been far easier than dealing with failure. Finally speaking up, he stated, "That's deep."

"You better believe it. It's life or death," Jerry agreed.

"I've heard of Christ before, but I'm not sure how I feel about him," Dom admitted. "The Christians I've been around in my life were legalistic hypocrites. I don't want to be like them." Dom shut his mouth, instantly feeling bad for lumping the gentle man sitting across from him in with all the Christians he had met in the past. Feeling uncomfortable,

Dom's knee started bouncing up and down.

In order to avoid eye contact, he began surveying Jerry's office. It was a tiny, dreary room with a short bookstand on the left side of the director's desk. On one of the dusty shelves, he saw a picture of Jerry and his family, which made Dom remember his circumstances. He realized that when all was said and done, this stranger was the only person on Earth who was treating him like a human being in need of compassion. This man cared more about Dom's family than anyone else appeared to.

Dom looked back at Jerry, finally cognizant that this Christian man was taking time out of his busy day to sit and share with him. Dom wished he could reel back the words he just spoke, like a fishing pole reels a hook back in from the water. He settled down and apologized to Jerry for being arrogant and judgmental.

Over the course of two more hours and three cups of coffee, Jerry proceeded to lay out Scriptures for Dom. He showed comfort and compassion rather than judgment or condemnation of his new friend. Once Dominic realized he was a sinner, just like everyone else, he accepted his need for a Savior and prayed to receive Christ into his heart.

Jerry smiled broadly, knowing he would spend eternity with his new brother, Dom.

Because he had made the most important decision of his life, Dominic La'Mone's name remained in the *book of life*, and the heavenly saints continued celebrating his conversion into God's family of believers.

Emma, on the other hand, had much to learn about life, death, faith, and God's amazing grace.

Chapter 8
Too Late

After Emma and the twins left Dom, they settled in her mother's home in Vancouver, Canada. Life in Vancouver certainly wasn't up to the standard of living they were accustomed to in America, but they had nowhere else to go.

Emma and her parents were originally from Alabama, but the large chemical company her father had worked for gave him a promotion and transferred him up north a little over two decades earlier. He died in an accident at work fifteen years later. Even though her mother had never told her so, Emma knew that the house must have been extremely quiet the past eleven years after Emma married and moved out.

Emma's mother, Pattie, told her that she was more than welcome to stay with her, and that she looked forward to having her daughter living with her again, as well as having the opportunity to get to know her grandchildren better.

To Emma, the home looked basically the same as she remembered it when she arrived at the age of five, except she noticed now that there were pictures and statues of Jesus all over the place, and her mother had covered the wall above the couch with different styles and colors of crosses.

"Mother," Emma said with contempt a few days after she and the kids were settled, "would you please explain all the Christian paraphernalia in the house?"

"Oh, dear, sit down," Pattie instructed joyfully. "I want to tell you something I'm really excited about." As she spoke, her mother sat down on the flowered sofa next to Emma and handed her a cup of hot tea.

"A couple weeks ago, my neighbor-friend took me to her church, and guess what happened?"

"I'm afraid to ask," Emma said sarcastically.

"I was born again!" Pattie exclaimed, throwing her hands up in the air triumphantly. Emma could do nothing but gape at her mother, who was reaching for her Bible that was lying on the glass-top coffee table in front of them. She couldn't believe what she had just heard.

"Mother, you know how I feel about that stuff!" she yelled. Ignoring the look of shock on Pattie's face, she bolted off the sofa and rushed out of the living room.

Emma had grown up in the *Bible Belt*. She knew all about being saved, getting baptized, spiritual gifts, and "Bible thumpers." She just couldn't find it in her heart to believe what she couldn't see. She wanted nothing to do with religion. In fact, in that moment, if she had somewhere else she and the kids could stay, she'd leave her mother's home and get her and her kids as far away from her mother's craziness as possible.

Feeling irritated with her mother, trapped by her circumstances, and disgusted with her life, Emma took to her bed and stayed there for three weeks. Grief and depression set in; she felt less of a woman due to Dominic's infidelity. Emma felt devoid of her dignity and lost in anger and resentment. She *still* couldn't get visions of her husband with other women out of her mind. She fantasized about what the other women in his secret fantasy life were like: Were they prettier than her? Smarter? Skinnier? Her runaway imagination tormented her with vivid pictures.

Her self-esteem was low, and she avoided going out in hopes that no one would recognize her. For that reason, Emma enrolled her son and daughter in a public elementary school within walking distance of her mother's home, so they pretty much took care of themselves. Over the following month, getting dressed, taking a bath, and making a cup of tea seemed like great accomplishments to her, while she continued to struggle with the highs and lows of grief.

The children noticed their mother's isolation and short temper. She seemed sad all the time and cried a lot. Simon and Alexandra noticed their mother wasn't spending time with them, helping them with homework, or eating with them. In fact, she wasn't eating much at all. Alexandra noticed her mother was the exact opposite of the young, vibrant, beautiful mother she knew in America. Similarly, Simon felt abandoned and sad over the loss of his dad and the distance of his mother. All of which, Emma overheard them telling her mother on numerous occasions, but she couldn't bring herself to leave her room.

Finally, Pattie, obviously fed up with her daughter's behavior, walked into Emma's childhood bedroom unannounced and said, "Em, this has got to stop." Her Southern twang seeped from every word. "You've got a college education. You've got two children who need you, and you've got to move on with your life."

"Noooo," Emma whined into her pillow, while her mother yanked the window shades open.

"You need to get dressed, young lady, work on a resume, and get a job. Do you hear me, Emma Jean?" Her mother spoke to her the way she had when she had been a little girl. Emma squinted from the sunlight shining into her eyes, but refused to move.

"Mother, I'm not a child!" she fumed.

"Well, you're acting like one! Now get up, get ready, and let's go to church."

"What day is it?" Emma whined again.

"Well, for crying out loud, it's Sunday! I'll get the kids some breakfast, and you get cleaned up."

"No, Mother!" Emma shouted. "I told you I wasn't interested in church. Do you hear me, Mother?"

"Oh, for Heaven's sake, Emma! I might not be able to drag you there, but I'm taking the kids. When we get back, I want you out of that bed, dressed, and looking through the want ads."

Thirty minutes later Emma heard car doors slamming as her mother and the kids left for church. *Finally, peace and quiet,* Emma thought just as the phone rang. She jolted with irritation.

"Hello!" she said gruffly, after roughly opening the cover of her cell phone.

"Is that you, Emma?" Dominic asked tenderly.

"I don't want to talk to you, Dom," she said as she started to close the phone.

"Wait, don't hang up," he begged. "I just wanted to check on you and the kids."

"We're fine," Emma said sharply.

There was a long pause and then Dom spoke up. "Listen, I want you to know I've gotten help. I'm sober now."

"What? You were drinking as well?" she asked with exasperation.

"No, that's a term we use in my therapy sessions. I've learned that I'm a sex addict, and the term *sober* means that I'm not acting out." There was silence over the line, while Emma tried to entertain what she was hearing. Dom continued. "I'm working hard, Emma, to get my life in order. I want my family back, I want you back, I want…"

Emma interrupted. "Listen, you've thrown my whole world upside down, Dom, and now you say you're addicted to sex? I don't understand any of this."

"I know, Em. I'm learning more about it, and about myself day by day." He sighed on the other end of the phone. "All I ask is that you forgive me someday for all I've done to you and the kids."

Emma didn't answer. She was still stewing over the whole situation, plus she was perplexed about the strange addiction Dom admitted to. In her mind, men thought about sex constantly, but she wondered if there could actually be such a thing as an addiction to it, or if this was just another one of Dom's pathetic lies.

After another period of silence, Emma finally spoke up. "Dom, do you really expect me to forgive you after all you've done to me? I lost my marriage, my home, my reputation, and my career path. I can barely go out in public anymore!"

"I understand it seems impossible right now, but I truly hope you can forgive me and learn to trust me again someday. I am so very sorry, Emma. It kills me that I hurt you so badly. I really messed up and lost control, but I've got a clear conscience now, Honey, before God and man."

"Oh no, not you, too!" Emma complained.

"Me too, what?"

"Please don't tell me you're on this God kick too. Mom has recently found religion and is off to church with the kids as we speak."

"Yes, I did. Actually, after you and the kids left, and we lost everything, I had nowhere else to go, so I started walking. I ended up at a homeless shelter and met this guy named Jeremiah. He helped me see the light when I could only see darkness all around me. He showed me God's Word that says all men fall short of the glory of the Lord. That's why we humans need the sacrificial Lamb. It was such a relief, Em, to know I wasn't the only sinner on this Earth.

"I can move on with my life knowing that no matter how badly I mess up, God still loves me and forgives me. It's amazing, Em! I'm happier than I've been in years—I mean, with my spiritual life. God is so good, Em. I accepted Him, and I've never felt so at peace in my entire life."

Emma was filing her nails while trying to figure out what a lamb had to do with anything. She really wanted to hang up and get back to sleep, but she remained quiet while Dom continued.

"Jerry, the man who shared redemption with me, has arranged for me to attend workshops for sex addicts. The counselors are helping me get to the root of my addiction. They are even helping me dig back to childhood wounds. Now I know I don't have to work so hard at being perfect, because no one is. And, Jesus loves me anyway. And Em, He wants our family back together…and so do I."

Emma wondered what childhood wound he was talking about. *Come on,* she thought, *everybody has scars from falling off their bikes, being scratched by a cat, or scraping themselves on the ce-*

ment. Wounds were normal in Emma's mind. She had never heard the term used the way he was using it before, plus she was in no mood to feel sorry for Dom, or even be happy about his conversion. Just the sound of his voice was starting to make her feel sick to her stomach.

"Well, it'll be a cold day in Hell before that happens," she said indignantly, pushing the end button on her cell phone as hard as she could. She knew she was being dramatic, but ending the call and pressing on the button with all her might somehow gave Em a feeling of power.

Emma didn't want to talk. She didn't want to think. She just wanted to sleep so she could dream about other people's lives and escape her own. And that's what she did for the next five days. All the while, her mother kept asking if she could locate a support group for her, or have her prayer chain pray for her, between bouts of hounding her about getting a job.

"It would really do you good to get out of here and go to church with us next Sunday," her mother said sweetly to her daughter one month after Emma's conversation with Dominic.

"Fine, Mother!" Emma snapped one day. "I'll make a deal with you. I'll go to church on Sunday, if you never, ever bring this subject up again. Okay? I'll go if you just shut up about this!"

Pattie grinned secretly, hoping next week's message would touch her daughter's heart. She so wanted Em to experience the comfort brought by fellowship with others.

However, a *prodigal son* experience didn't happen that following Sunday. Emma sat with her arms crossed and her lips pursed while sneering at the pastor, the worship choir, and the folks who tried to greet her after the service.

Her heart was cold and hardened to God. She thought of him merely as a menacing force that swooped down and damned people to Hell when they didn't behave. She could picture him striking her with lightning every time she said a curse word, or thumping her over the head when she thought something mean about someone.

Emma wasn't interested in hearing about his love either, especially now that her experience with Dom had her questioning everything she had ever believed about the subject.

Once the service was *finally* over, and the four of them reached the car, Emma stopped to glare at her mother, and asked, "Are you happy? I went, now leave me alone!" She slid into the front seat of her mother's four-door sedan and remained silent all the way home.

Later she overheard Simon and Alexandra telling their grandmother how embarrassed they were at how immature their mother was acting. Going to church didn't seem to be that big of a deal to them. Of course, they had no idea what she was really going through.

Upon arriving at her mother's house, Emma once again settled into her room, ignoring the rest of the family. She couldn't help feeling self-focused while thoughts bombarded her mind. *What if Dom exposed me to sexually transmitted diseases? What if he gave me AIDS? What if he had a love child with one of his perfect, little, sex kittens?*

I just want to sleep, Emma thought, so she looked through the medicine cabinet in her bathroom and found something to relax her. *Hmmm, I'm supposed to take one pill every eight hours,* she thought, reading the instructions on the side of the bottle. *I wonder if I'd sleep longer if I took three.* She reached for a glass of water, threw her head back to get the pills down her throat, then lay down in her childhood bed snuggling into her pillows.

While closing her eyes to rest, Emma was oblivious to trouble brewing just around the corner. An eighteen-year-old boy and his buddies had just stolen a Dodge Ram pickup and were speeding through the nearby neighborhoods. The four were drinking heavily, and the driver was showing off by carelessly speeding through the narrow streets. His cell phone rang, and, as he reached down, he lost control of the truck, jumped a curb, and slammed into the exterior wall of the bedroom Emma was sleeping in. She died instantly.

When Emma woke up, her room was pitch-black. Sitting up in bed, she noticed it was too dark to see her hands in front of her face. Em got out of bed and reached for the walls to help her feel her way to the powder room. Step by step, she stumbled along the thick carpet while her hands felt for windows, doorways, and, eventually, the bathroom sink.

She had made it through the doorjamb of the powder room when instead of feeling the towel rack, she felt cold steel, vertical bars, like the ones in a jail cell. *That's strange*, she thought, *my bathroom doesn't feel like that.*

She wondered if she was walking in her sleep when she moved her hands around again trying to feel her way. In her wildest dreams, she would have never guessed what would happen next. Her fingers touched what felt like a person's nose!

"Who is in my bathroom?" Emma called out while shrieking in horror.

"Who's there?" the deep stranger's voice called out.

Emma reacted with another high-pitched scream. "Get out of my room, you pervert!" she shouted.

"Your room?" the man snorted. "Get out of my way, Newbie!"

She tried moving away, but, as she shifted, she ran into another body. "Agh!" she screamed. "What's going on? Why is it so dark and cold in here? And what is that putrid smell?"

For a brief second, she wondered if the pipes were backing up in her restroom. Em was shifting again to head in another direction when something grabbed her. She was suddenly being shaken and beaten mercilessly by some kind of reptile-like being that towered over her. She could feel its rough scales and sharp claws as it slapped her face and punched her body. All the while, it screamed hideously with delight.

Then Em felt an enormous reptile begin to wrap itself around her and then morph into a serpent that was squeezing the life out of her. Every bone in her body was being compressed to the point of breaking. Emma felt like she was going to throw up, or that she would pass out at any moment.

Once it finally let loose, she fell to the floor and got away from the vicious creature by crawling as fast as she could, but she couldn't find her way out of the darkness, not to mention she was disoriented, bruised, and hurting. The beast must have transformed back into a two-legged creature with arms, because it grabbed her again, pulled her backwards, and then forced her to stand as the blows to her body continued.

Emma could hear the sounds of crowds of people around her laughing, cursing, and cheering. She felt like she was the main attraction of a boxing match she was bound to lose. Squealing with delight, the freakishly tall creature tore at her skin with its claws, while Emma screamed uncontrollably.

Finally, the beating stopped. She lay face down on cold cement with tears flowing down her cheeks. Emma could tell the violence had ended because she heard a different poor soul in another part of the area wailing from the torture he was receiving. She had never felt such pain in her life. She laid in the dark for a long time, working through the shock of what had just happened to her.

Once her breathing slowed, Emma realized her right foot had broken when the beast stepped on it, plus many of her ribs felt fractured. She presumed her face was scratched pretty badly, considering the amount of pain she felt every time she blinked her eyes, and by the amount of blood she could feel running down her neck.

Why is this happening? Emma wondered. While she cried and sobbed, a voice yelled, "Shut up!" And then other voices from men and women of all ages around her chimed in; they were saying cruel things to her and coming closer to kick at her. Emma still couldn't see a thing, not even her hands held out in front of her. She needed help getting out of the area, but she couldn't tell where she was, or who was around her. It was the most frighteningly brutal experience she had ever gone through in her life.

"Where am I? What happened to my bedroom?" she moaned aloud.

"You're in Sheol…Hades…Hell, Princess," a young man's voice next to her said snidely.

Emma began shaking. *If I am in Hell, I must be dead! It can't be! There are so many things I still want to do! I want to attend my children's high school graduations, I want to help them visit colleges, plan their weddings, hold my grandchildren, and travel the world.*

She thought back and realized she must have taken too many pills that evening. Perhaps she *was* in Hell; Heaven certainly couldn't be what she was experiencing. *It must be true! What the pastor said about life and death this morning was true!* she thought regretfully.

"I want out of here!" she shrieked at the top of her voice. "Get me out of here…" Emma jumped, feeling someone grab her arm and start to lead her away from the cell. She was hopping on one foot, moaning, and holding her painful rib cage while trying to keep up. The overindulged woman had never experienced such sheer agony in her entire life.

"See that?" the strange woman asked once she had escorted Emma to a trace of light. Emma strained her eyes and finally saw red-hot flames in the distance. She staggered forward with the stranger until she could see movement. What she witnessed looked like the projection of a horror movie. Monsters and reptile-like beings that seemed twelve feet tall were chasing people around and whipping them. There was no end to the screeching and wailing of those surrounding her.

The female spoke up again, saying, "See that pit? Jump in there, and get it over with." The area was louder than the one Emma was previously in. There was screaming, moaning, yelling, and beatings going on in every direction.

"Get what over with?" Emma yelled over the chaotic noise at the grayish-looking woman who appeared to be in her forties.

"The pain, dummy!"

Emma looked further ahead and saw a deep pit filled with swirling flames and gray smoke. Looking down inside it, she could see people hovering in it who were moaning and burning. The smell was horrific. Emma looked away; she couldn't stand the sight of it. The heat from it made her thirsty. *I can hardly breathe*, she thought, brushing sweat from her brow.

"It's so hot in here. My throat is parched. Do you have any water?" she tried asking the repulsive woman who had led her near the pit. The stranger laughed at her and smugly answered, "There's no water here! Of course it's hot, it's Hell, you idiot!"

"How can I get out of here?" Emma begged loudly.

"Jump in the hole!" the strange lady instructed. Emma was willing to do anything to escape the horror. She hopped closer to look further into the pit, and, when she did, a shrieking demon approached her rapidly.

Jumping out of desperation, she fell and fell, and then the flames consumed her. It was nightmarish. This pain was worse than anything she had felt up to this point in her life. She wanted the pain to stop—her body to die—but it wouldn't. Emma's body kept burning, yet somehow she was living through the torturous, never-ending suffering.

She heard the woman who had instructed her to jump laughing from up above the bottomless pit. "Ha, ha, tricked you!" she said, cackling like the Wicked Witch of the West from the *Wizard of Oz*.

"Help me! Somebody, help me," Emma shrieked at the top of her lungs. Bodies of other people seemed to hover around her. There was no exit for any of them. No escape. No way to climb out of the pit.

"Dominic, help!" she begged, but he didn't come to her rescue. There appeared to be no hero diving in to save her. Emma was terrified and couldn't imagine living like this for eternity. She remembered the sermon she had heard that very morning and yelled, "God…if you're real, save me!"

The scariest voice she had ever heard bellowed through the dungeon. The sounds reverberated in ripple effects as it asked, "Who said that?" She looked up, and several bright white spotlights shone on a black, hideous creature standing at the brim of the pit. It stood upright and appeared to be around eighteen feet tall! He reminded Emma of a raven with a wingspan of eight feet long, and under each of his four wings were what looked like the hands of a man.

The creature was larger than the other beasts, and it commanded attention, as if it was in charge. If Emma had to guess, she would have bet it was the prince of the power of the air—Satan.

Black, evil spirits pointed menacingly down into the pit, affirming that Emma was the one who called out to God. The demons were then ordered to use steel cables to reach down to Emma. They helped her slip into a harness; her broken foot dangled freely back and forth, and the cables caused further pain to her already painful rib cage. The freakish demon beings were uninterested in her plight while hoisting Em up from the fiery pit.

At first, Emma was naïve enough to think they were having mercy on her, but once they had her broken, charred body on the surface, she realized their evil motives. They were presenting their captive to the dastardly corrupt devil who was waiting to confront her instead.

He drew close to her small frame. Emma had to strain to stare up at the towering figure looming over her. Before turning her face from him, she noted that he not only had four wings, but he had four faces too! Satan's entire body, including his back, his hands, and his wings, was completely full of repugnant looking eyes.

To her, the crow-like beast reeked of evil. Everything from his menacing looking eyeballs to his repulsive demeanor screamed arrogance and lack of control. Without him saying a word, Emma could tell this being despised her and wanted nothing more than to see her squirm in pain.

The devil leaned down and one of his hideous distorted faces came within inches of Emma's pretty face. She felt as if his piercing eyes could see inside to her very soul, and she could feel the heat of his breath on her forehead.

"Did you dare call out for God in my presence?" he demanded in a loud, deep, raspy tone. She couldn't pick one sole eyeball to focus in on while responding to his growling persona. Each one looked in different directions—some of the grotesque, protruding eyeballs were keeping an eye on each and every one of his henchmen, and each of the other beady little eyes watched each of his captured souls. He had the ability to scour every millimeter of his kingdom at all times. To Em, it appeared as if the devil was insecure and vulnerable; therefore, his lack of trust kept him on guard at all times.

He circled her like prey; Emma looked around with great trepidation. She was deathly afraid of him, yet still she found the strength to whisper, "Yes." She wanted to run and hide instead. She would give anything to be somewhere else… millions of miles away from the predator who was mocking her.

"This is my domain!" he roared at her, leaning in close to her face again. Her ears were pounding from the force of the monstrous sound he made. Emma cringed in fear, and then braced herself for an attack by placing her arms over her head.

"Never, ever, say that name again!" He cursed and shouted at her, then he gestured to his cronies, who dragged out a heavy, charred, wooden cross to tie Emma's tortured and beaten body to. She tried kicking at the ugly black demons with her one good foot to resist them, but she was no match for their strength. Emma was screaming in severe pain and begging for mercy while they brutally hung her on the cross and hoisted her high for all to see.

"This is what happens when you bow to any other than me," Lucifer announced loudly to Hell's inhabitants. Hell was quiet for the first time since she had arrived, as the residents of Hades watched Emma squirm. A second spotlight shone on her; her eyes squinted, her shoulders slumped, and her head drooped. Emma La'Mone was made a spectacle for Lucifer's entire imprisoned kingdom to see.

Satan began laughing hysterically. He pranced and danced while he circled his newly captured prize.

Over and over he bellowed, "You're never getting out of here Emma Jean! You're mine—you'll never be rid of me! You had your chance to choose the King of Kings and you didn't take it—shamey, shamey!" wagging his ugly, deformed finger in her face.

"Now you get to live here with me forever and ever in *my* kingdom," he ridiculed and provoked. Emma knew it was too late for her. She wished she could go back to warn Simon and Alexandra about the reality of Hell. She wished she could see their faces one more time. Never in her life had she contemplated living in the synagogue of the counterfeit god—Satan. Yet, here she was forevermore.

Lucifer, the devil, continued howling and bellowing. "It's too late, Emma Jean!" His words and laughter echoed hauntingly through the chambers, reminding her of Vincent Price's sinister laugh at the end of Michael Jackson's video, *Thriller*. She had heard it for the first time when she was in middle school, and could have never guessed then how it would taunt her now–Bhah ha ha ha ha…Bhah ha ha ha ha ha ha ha.

Chapter 9
Second Chances

By now, you're probably wondering how the souls in section 8:22 a.m. saw Emma La'Mone's body entering the gates of Heaven earlier in this story, while you've just read about her being in Hell. Actually, what really happened is that she took way too many pills that night, which caused her to have a horrific nightmare—fortunately. That Hell she thought she experienced was only a bad dream.

The very next morning, Emma writhed in her bed and kicked at the pretty, pink sheets. Her pajama top was soaked from a great deal of perspiration, and she felt weak—almost as if she had been fighting with someone or something all night long.

"No, stop…someone help me!" she yelled desperately.

Hearing screams, Pattie ran into Emma's bedroom, tried to calm her daughter down, and coax her awake. In that foggy place between dreams and reality, Emma continued to scream in a voice slowly going hoarse in protest to her mother's hands touching her. Em's brain had not registered that she was no longer wrestling with a demon or Satan, so she fought against her mother, accidentally scratching her face.

Pattie yelled loud enough that Emma finally opened her eyes. Her mother was standing over the edge of her bed, her hand over the left side of her face where Emma had scratched her. The shock of seeing fear and pain on her mother's face calmed her, but it didn't do much to alleviate her initial confusion. Slowly, she groggily surveyed her childhood bedroom and then burst out crying with joy.

Overwhelming comfort and thankfulness welled up inside her when she realized the dark heaviness of the nightmare she had during the night wasn't real; she was free from the cold, metal shackles in her dream.

The twins fearfully poked their heads into Emma's room, but Pattie shooed them away. She couldn't bear the thought of her innocent grandchildren seeing their mother like that.

"Mother, is it really you?" Em asked hopefully, sitting up in bed and wiping the tears from her eyes.

"Yes, Honey, it's me. Are you fully awake now?" Pattie asked, hesitantly stepping toward her daughter.

When her mother was within arm's length, Emma grabbed her and held her as tight as she could. The two of them rocked back and forth on Emma's bed, as tears of relief, mixed with rivers of sorrow over what could have been, streamed down Em's face.

"What in the world are you so upset about, Sweetheart?" Pattie asked, rubbing her daughter's back in the soothing motherly way mamas do.

Once she composed herself, Emma replied, "Mom, I dreamt I was in Hell. It was so real. I could actually feel the pain as what seemed like a ferocious reptile brutally beat me.

Then it morphed into what felt like a large, constricting viper."

Pattie's forehead furled at the thought of what that would feel like.

"I wanted to be rid of the pain they were causing me, so I jumped into a pit of flames. I thought if I jumped into the pit my body would die, but it wouldn't! I couldn't escape, Mom! My body kept burning. And that was just the beginning. Satan and his evil demons tied me to a cross, and laughed while I suffered through more agonizing pain. There was no escape," Em said with anguish. "I called out for help, but not even God could save me. It was too late!" she said, looking at her mother through a different lens than the night before.

Again, the eight-year-old twins timidly peeked their heads into their mother's room. They were both afraid after hearing the commotion coming from her bedroom.

They knew something was extremely wrong since their grandmother had made them both leave the room. This time Pattie reassured them that their mother had experienced an upsetting nightmare, but she would be just fine. Pattie gently sent them off into the kitchen to make peanut butter toast.

Once they were gone, Emma continued to share every detail of the dream with her mother, and then asked her to call her pastor for a meeting. Pattie could understand why her daughter was so upset about the nightmare. Emma seemed legitimately scared to death. Feeling stunned by her daughter's change of heart, Pattie called Pastor Kelley immediately. Luckily, he had a counseling session cancel that morning, so he told her to bring Emma right over to his office at the church.

Since the twins were not old enough to stay home alone, Pattie asked her neighbor to come over and sit with them.

She then helped her daughter dress and drove her to the church she frequented. Emma greeted the portly, redheaded clergyman and apologized for being so distant and rude at the service the day before. Pastor Kelley understood and gestured for her to have a seat in his wood-paneled office, and then he invited her to tell him what was on her mind.

Emma gave him a brief rundown of her history with Dominic, her family's stay in America, the separation, and how she ended up living with her mother. She then described the anger, bitterness, and fear she had been dealing with over it all. Pastor Kelley was familiar with the characteristics of grief, so he wasn't surprised to hear that Emma struggled with her self-esteem, with depression, and with wanting to alienate herself from the rest of her family, as well as the world, due to Dominic's blatant betrayal.

Emma then revealed the tangible evil of the nightmare to him while he listened earnestly. She described feeling lonely, eternally separated from God, and hopeless in Hell. She characterized the devil to the pastor, and told him how Satan had ordered his henchmen to tie her to a rugged cross and display her body for all of Hades' inhabitants to see.

When she finished her tale, Pastor Kelley shook his head and said in his deep, Irish accent, "Emma, I've got to tell you that what you've described amazingly resembles the Hell people who have had near-death experiences have told me about."

"What are you saying?" Emma asked, confused and worried that maybe she had somehow overdone it with the pills and had actually died for a brief second. Then deciding that couldn't be it, she wondered if God had somehow given her the vision to help set her on the path he wanted her on.

"I'm telling you that Hell does exist." He reached for his Bible and showed her verses found in the New Testament. Putting on thick glasses, the kind man read: "Matthew 10:28 in the NIV says, 'Do not be afraid of those who kill the body but cannot kill the soul. Rather, be afraid of the One who can destroy both soul and body in hell.' " Pastor Kelley looked up at Emma, and then he waited patiently for her to absorb what he just read.

Feeling confident that the verse had not confused her, he continued reading. "Emma, Matthew 7:13 also tells us that wide is the gate and broad is the road that leads to destruction and many enter into it. On the other hand, small is the gate and narrow is the road that leads to life, and only a few find it. I have to wonder if God allowed you to have this dream to get your attention—to make you realize you were on the wrong path. He clearly doesn't want a single soul to perish."

Emma nodded in agreement, visibly wanting to steer clear from any and everything related to the devil or Hell.

"I personally believe God's love goes beyond human understanding. I believe He gives people chances to reciprocate his love until the very moment that it is literally too late," the kind man offered.

Emma scratched her head and asked, "Are you saying He is giving me a second chance?" She inwardly prayed this was the case.

"It's quite possible," the pastor said. "He loves you so much, Dear. He won't take you home until you've had every last chance to accept, or fully deny, Him."

"I cried out to Him in my dream Pastor Kelley. I wanted to be with Him so badly. I can't stand the thought of living, *or* dying, without Him," Emma cried.

"Would you like to pray to receive Him into your heart once and for all?" the minister asked excitedly.

"Yes, I want to give my life to Jesus," Emma replied closing her eyes in eager anticipation.

"Dear Heart, repeat after me," he said soberly.

Emma's relief at the opportunity to choose her future residence brought her to her knees. She confessed her sins, and then echoed his words verbatim.

"Lord, please forgive me of my sins. I'm tired of doing it my way, and I want you to take over and be my Lord and Savior. Please come into my life and show me how you want me to live. Amen."

After praying, Emma felt relieved and free...free from the pressure of life's burdens...free from trying to save her self...secure in her destiny. She knew her heart changed forever, because she felt as though a warm light pierced into her very soul, filling the emptiness with peace and well-being.

When Emma stood to leave, the clergyman gave her a Bible. The broad smile on her face and twinkle in her lovely, green eyes indicated to Pastor Kelley that she eagerly anticipated getting to learn all about Elohim, her Creator.

Once they returned home, Pattie reminded her daughter that being saved from Hell didn't mean things would automatically be perfect in her life. She would still struggle with sin, but she would have the Bible to lead her, plus the Holy Spirit's counsel and guidance. She told Emma that knowing of Jesus' extravagant love, mercy, and grace would give her the joy and peace to get through each and every trial, big or small.

The following day, Emma called and talked to Dominic. She found out that he had been saving his money to fly to Canada to try to reconcile with her. Her heart had softened and she, too, wanted her family back together again. She would never forget the betrayal he caused her; yet, she had decided to forgive her husband, as Christ had forgiven her of her transgressions. Instead of living in the past, she decided to focus on the future.

Dom told her he would be done with his counseling sessions in two weeks, and that's when he planned on moving back to Canada. They both agreed that it would be best if he rented an apartment while they resurrected their broken marriage by dating each other again.

Dom suggested that it might be a good idea for Em to see a counselor herself to work on the issues she was dealing with due to his adultery. Emma was further relieved that he understood and appreciated the range of emotions that made her feel like she was going crazy half of the time.

Emma looked forward to her husband moving back and mending their torn and tattered marriage. After ending their call, she gave thanks to God for sparing her family from an ugly divorce.

For the first time in months, Emma felt like she was living again, this time with less vanity or need for riches or fame. She felt carefree while walking the kids to school each day. She was even beginning to notice little things, like the sound of the birds singing, the picturesque snow-capped mountains that she could see in the distant landscape near her mother's home, red and black ladybugs crawling on the flower petals blooming in the neighbor's garden, and how life was so precious and short. Emma was especially thankful that she got a choice as to where she would spend eternity.

Two weeks later, after escorting the children to school, Emma started walking the short distance home. She was talking to God and thanking Him for the multicolored sunrise on the horizon. Today it was in purples and pinks, whereas yesterday's was in oranges and yellows. Emma read in her Bible that Christ paints every morning sunrise differently. The thought of it made her smile. She chuckled, thinking how she was now one of the "Bible thumpers" she used to despise.

Now that Emma stopped to think about it, she realized that reading the Word gave her purpose and hope. She found answers to all of life's questions in it. Em was starting to see how the One who was the resurrection and the life had taken the time to leave an instruction manual to guide people through life. Following it made her feel more confident in her decisions, and keener to help the people around her.

It was becoming more and more evident to her that even though God was immensely sovereign, He created people for His pleasure. From what she read about Him, He seemed to be interested in small details, such as designing each and every person specifically, down to different looks, fingerprints, DNA, and even distinct pupils. He seemed to be incredibly creative in her eyes.

While continuing to daydream, Em found herself wondering how God told flowers when to bloom, or how He told whales when to migrate, or bears when to hibernate. Such things she had never really paid attention to, or given much thought about, before.

Walking along, she then began thinking about having her family together soon. Dominic had finished his counseling sessions and earned enough at his job helping Jerry at the homeless shelter to fly to Canada to reunite with her and the kids. She was thinking about seeing his face again after nearly six months, when she walked into the street from behind a school bus.

Another mother, who had just dropped off her children, didn't see her through the rising sun that was shining into her eyes. Her silver luxury sedan slammed into Emma. There was a loud thump, and Em's body flew several feet.

The distraught driver began to scream and cry. She jumped out of her car and ran to the injured woman's side. Kneeling down, she placed her arm under Em's neck, lifting her a bit to search for a pulse and listen to hear if she was breathing.

The hysterical woman was crying; her eyes looking up and around for someone to help her. While holding the slumped woman's body, the distressed driver looked down at Em's face, crying, "Please, wake up! I didn't see you. I didn't mean to hurt you. Just please, please wake up!"

Emma's eyes fluttered, and then finally opened slowly, yet only halfway. She was groggy and confused, feeling the effects of the painful ordeal. Looking into Em's glazed eyes, the remorseful woman repeated hysterically, "I'm so sorry, I didn't see you!"

Emma could feel her body and mind somehow slipping away. She could hear the woman holding her crying, but she felt no desire to get up, recap what happened, or move on with her life. Instead, with all the strength she could muster, and though mortally wounded, she managed to part her dry, parched lips and whisper, "I forgive you," giving the distraught driver the pardon she desperately longed for. Immediately, Em let go of her earthly life, closed her eyes, and fell asleep.

By now, a crowd of strangers was huddled around the two women, asking what happened and how they could help. Without a reply, the troubled driver hovering over the deceased woman closed her eyes and inwardly begged the Lord to forgive her for taking the life of this beautiful stranger—Emma La'Mone.

This time when Emma opened her eyes upon her demise, she was standing in front of the glorious, radiant, holy *judgment seat*. Death had no sting—it was sheer beauty compared to the horror of the nightmare she had experienced a few months earlier. Again, thankfulness overflowed from her heart when she realized what she had nearly missed.

Chapter 10
The Room of Gifts

Teresa's head hung low after leaving the *room of files* and joining the other souls from section 8:06 a.m. in the *holding area*. She noticed that the big guy named Anthony was back too, but Victoria Valentine, her daughter's favorite star, was not. Teresa figured that she was still in the *room of files*.

Teresa's heart was heavy with the reminder of the many people who had loved her in the past, as well as how deeply God adored her, but she just couldn't get past some of her expectations. She wanted to be loved more than anything in the world, yet she wanted it on her terms.

To her, the love needed to be physically tangible, such as a hug or a kiss from a human being. She wanted to be able to see and touch the One she pledged her heart to. Also, if she *did* choose to return God's love, she wanted Him all to herself—she didn't want to share Him with billions of others.

While Teresa was standing near the glass, wrestling with her emotions, Maxine, the blabbermouth, walked up, took her by the arm, and began to gossip some more about the people in their section. Teresa was in no mood to listen, but she was unable to break free from the hefty woman's tight grip.

"Did you know that Herb, the pilot, has a swastika tattoo on his forearm?" Maxine asked in a pseudo-whisper, spinning Teresa around to face the man. She didn't even wait for a response from the clearly annoyed woman though before blurting out, "I also heard that a famous leader of al-Qaeda is in section 8:31 a.m. I haven't seen him yet. Have you seen him?"

Teresa had to practically pull her arm out of its socket to free herself from the woman's grasp. She tried to ignore Maxine. She didn't want to be privy to her scandalous rumors. Instead, she looked around her section and was relieved to see that Victoria was back from the *room of files*.

Teresa wanted to walk over, introduce herself properly this time, and talk about the fan club Lupita had developed for the young superstar. Heading in her direction, Teresa saw that a group of autograph seekers was already beginning to surround the famous beauty, so she sat back down on one of the numerous benches and looked out the glass instead.

For the first time since she had returned from the *room of files*, Teresa noticed that what she was seeing on the other side of the glass was moving ever so slowly again, so she guessed her section was moving along the corridor. Sitting on the bench and marveling at how the slight movement felt like she was floating brought a smile to Teresa's disgruntled face. *It was certainly a smooth transition from one area to the next,* she thought.

Even though the changing scenery was awe-inspiring, it failed to hold her attention. She hated to admit it, but she couldn't contain her curiosity about the al-Qaeda leader Maxine had mentioned. Teresa wanted to know if the villain Maxine told her about was indeed in section 8:31 a.m. She found herself wondering if it was one of the tyrants she had seen in the headlines the last couple years.

Teresa tried to appear inconspicuous as she nonchalantly stood up and began dragging her broken leg over to the clear partition separating her section from the ones behind hers. Peering through the glass, she tried to see through the throngs of people if the man was the infamous leader of the terrorist network that killed thousands of innocent people in New York City that horrible day a decade ago. Unfortunately, the crowd in that section was too large to see through. She gave up and sat back down on a nearby bench.

It seemed like only moments later when Teresa's section came to a gentle stop, and, once again, hundreds of doors in the glass sides of the enclosure lifted high. More mighty angel-men appeared from each doorway to escort each of the souls to his or her own *room of gifts.*

Each person in section 8:06 a.m. exited until Teresa and the famous starlet were the only two left standing in the *holding area.*

"Teresa Hernandez, please follow me," the everchivalrous, kind being, standing in front of her in the doorway leading to her *room of gifts,* called. Teresa obediently followed the angel-man, while she pondered what in the world the *room of gifts* was going to be like.

Last, but not least, Vickie Ann Songtrot, who had waited because she wanted to make a grand entrance, sauntered over to her awaiting angel. When her escort announced her name, Vickie became quite annoyed that her professional name, Victoria Valentine, wasn't being used in this strange place. Choosing to ignore the insult, the gorgeous young star composed herself, arched her back, stuck out her chest, and walked toward the door marked *room of gifts,* as if she were walking the red carpet.

The talented actress entered the enormous room and burst out laughing. "I knew it!" giggled Victoria. "This is a surprise party, isn't it? My agent planned it, right?" She squealed as her lovely hazel eyes took in the grandiose room, lined floor to ceiling with shelves. Presents wrapped in gorgeous paper, bows, and ribbons adorned the hundreds of shelves. She saw silver boxes, presents wrapped in gold paper, and some with red and blue ribbons decorating their tops; practically every color she could imagine adorned the spacious area.

Vickie was thoroughly elated when she saw that there were thousands of these brightly decorated gifts, each with the name Vickie Ann Songtrot on them. *Wait a minute,* Victoria thought. *None of my friends or fans knows my real name.* This meant that this was a private, family party of some kind. The day wasn't her birthday, but she could think of no other reason her mother, father, and siblings would throw her a party. Maybe they missed her and this was their way of begging her to come around more often. She decided she would wait and see how the party went before deciding.

Even though every part of her wanted to rush to the nearest box and rip it open, she made herself patiently wait for her family members to pop out and yell, "Surprise!" But the room remained silent.

"Okay, somebody help me. I need a ladder. I want to start with that big one right there," Victoria announced, pointing her perfectly manicured finger at a shiny silver box glistening with glitter and red bows five shelves up, right in front of her.

"Vickie, do you know where you are?" a disembodied voice asked from a speaker above the door like the one in the *room of files.* She was startled, though she recognized the Voice coming from above her as the one that called to her in the *holding area*. She looked around for the first time and noticed the height and depth of the shelves, neatly lined with unopened presents. There were no windows in the room except the clear ceiling above her. She was all alone in the area, which made her feel certain people were hiding somewhere, ready to jump out at her even though she couldn't see any place in the room for them to actually hide in.

"Well, I think I'm at a surprise party!" she responded gleefully. "Oh, and by the way, would you please call me Victoria?"

"Victoria, open the bright pink and green polka-dotted gift right in front of you." The box the Voice spoke of was located two boxes over on the same shelf as the silver box with red bows that she pointed at earlier.

Victoria eagerly reached for the box and tore it open, as if she were an excited four-year-old child at Christmas time. She found a light blue silk sash inside the box with the word *Humility* embroidered on it.

"Is this a joke?" Vickie asked. "What am I supposed to do with this?" Annoyed, she threw it to the side and eagerly reached for another gift that someone had wrapped in gold and burgundy velvet. Ripping off the lid, another silk banner lay inside that read *Kindness.*

Victoria frowned and asked with indignation in her voice, "Who gives boring, ridiculous gifts like this?"

"God does," the Voice coming over the speaker answered.

Victoria looked confused. God had never been part of her life. She had everything she could ever want; therefore, she really had no use for him. She pondered why anyone would send her presents from a *distant somebody* she chose not to accept.

Suddenly, the Voice interrupted her thoughts. "Vickie, you overdosed this morning. Do you remember mixing vodka and methamphetamines?"

"Yes, I do it all the time...what do you mean I over... dosed," she stuttered, recalling her morning ritual. "Where am I?" she asked, while surveying the area in bewilderment as if seeing it for the first time.

"Victoria, it's true. You died this morning, and now God is giving you an overview of your life," the Voice said considerately. "You were in the *holding area* gazing upon the beauty of Heaven, and now you are in your private *room of gifts.*"

Vickie sat down on a row of gifts, effectively squashing them, and thought for a long while about what the Voice had just told her. She remembered waking up late and feeling rushed to get to a photo shoot for an expensive perfume company. She knew they would be furious with her if she didn't show up on time, and she didn't feel like dealing with the pressure or the guilt. Since she had gotten high before photo shoots in the past, and found that it made her more relaxed and photogenic, she decided to try it again.

When her boyfriend stopped by her apartment to pick her up that morning, he wanted to celebrate his new role in a major motion picture, so the two shared some vodka. She didn't think mixing the two drugs would affect her; after all, she did it all the time. It was really no big deal in her opinion.

Why does this know-it-all have to come along and try to spoil my fun? she thought. *He is such a killjoy!*

Feeling cocky and overly confident, Vickie decided she was going to play games with the Voice. *He couldn't prove she was dead, or that God existed*, she thought. So she exclaimed, "There is no God! You either have good luck or bad luck.

People like me have good luck," she said with obvious conceit in her voice.

"Anyway, I can't be dead—my horoscope said today was my lucky day!" She flipped her head arrogantly, scoffed, and then laughed haughtily.

When her words received no reply from the Voice, Vickie stood and said, "See!" She was pulling her necklace around her neck and pointing a horseshoe pendant outlined in diamonds up toward where the sound of the Voice had come from. Still tipsy and feeling the effects of the meth and alcohol, she suddenly lost her balance and fell into a pile of boxes adorning the floor next to where she had been standing. Her glittery, dark blue, party dress wrinkled up to her thighs and one of her stiletto pumps flew off her foot and popped the lid off another one of the gifts. A light pink banner saying *Charity* slid out.

Victoria reached over, picked up the sash, stood, and proudly placed an end over one shoulder, and the other around her waist. She acted as if she was modeling it while saying glibly, "Hey, I like this one. I give to charity all the time!"

"You gave money to save the whales, Victoria, but God created them, and He is perfectly capable of taking care of them Himself. God wanted you to give your money to *people* who needed it. He wanted you to help your parents in Madison, instead of allowing them to lose their home once your father was laid off. He wanted you to have compassion for the homeless couple that stood outside of your apartment building every day. Instead, you laughed and mocked them by throwing dog biscuits toward them."

Vickie didn't even have the decency to feel ashamed at the words; she just continued pretending she was modeling her sash while prancing around the spacious area like a beauty queen.

"Victoria," the Voice continued tenderly, "look around and see the many shapes and sizes of the gifts on the shelves."

Of course, the prideful starlet pretended like she wasn't interested, so she only half-glanced at the shelves surrounding her.

"Blessings come in all shapes and sizes, Precious Girl. For instance, by helping your parents financially, you may have received a reward from God in the form of inner peace, contentment, or self-fulfillment. Or, He might have blessed you financially, physically, or emotionally, for God loves the heart of a cheerful giver.

"Likewise, by helping the homeless couple, you would have planted a seed of concern, compassion, and thoughtfulness that you would have reaped later on in your own life—for what you reap, you sow. Some people think of it as karma, or 'what comes around goes around'. Basically, the effects of doing the right thing are always positive in God's eyes.

"Similarly, the Lord wanted you to give to missionaries and the church…"

"Wait a moment," Vickie rudely infringed. "If God's broke, he can't expect me to save the world! Uh-uh," she said, wagging her finger back and forth.

"No, you've missed the point," the Voice said gingerly. "God doesn't need your money. He isn't jealous of your success, wealth, or popularity. In fact, your musical talent, acting ability, and beauty were *gifts* from Him. God isn't jealous *of* you. No, He's jealous *for* your attention and your love," the Voice said sweetly. "He created you for so much more than stardom. He designed you to be giving, selfless, and faithful. That's what all these gifts were all about. He wanted to grace you with gifts of many kinds, including hope, joy, peace…"

"Look, Mister," Vickie interrupted again. "I have faith in myself. Okay. I'm happy with me. I trust me. I don't need no god coming along and telling me I'm not good enough, or I'm not this or I'm not that. Who does he think he is?"

"You were created perfectly in God's eyes, Victoria. God designed you holy and without a fault, but without Him in your life, you experienced a void in your heart only He could fill. Wine, men, success, drugs, and fame couldn't fill that void. He wanted to save you from yourself so you could experience a joy money couldn't buy."

Victoria rolled her eyes, looking away haughtily.

"My child," the Voice continued, "God gave you the resources to store up your treasures in Heaven."

"Ummm, I don't know if you noticed, but I have all the treasures I need," Vickie said sarcastically, placing her hands on her hips. She started making a mental list of all the material wealth she had accumulated over the last couple years. *Let's see, there's the house in France, the summer home in Florida, the Jaguar…*

"Victoria, did you use your fortune to help people in need? Did you volunteer your time to organizations that were helping those who couldn't help themselves? Did you use your platform to tell others about the attributes of the Lord, or did you use your celebrity to exalt yourself?" the Voice asked politely.

There was silence in the room and then Victoria spoke up. "You know what? Now that I think about it, your God is mean. You say he loves me unconditionally, and then you bring me here and say he withheld all of these things from me," she said, gesturing toward the shelves of presents. "That's just wrong!"

"What God really wanted was to gift you with a relationship with Him," the Voice said compassionately.

Vickie laughed. "So, you're saying I was supposed to walk around talking to my 'imaginary friend,' " Vickie said sarcastically as her fingers gestured quotation marks. "I can just picture the tabloid pictures now. No thanks—I think I'll pass!"

Just then, the floor opened in front of her and a solid gold, square pedestal lifted up slowly from the floor. Vickie's hazel eyes grew wide with dismay and curiosity while she inched closer to it. She looked like a small child coveting the contents of a cookie jar while she salivated over the sweet prize inside. Perched on the stand was a four-sided, crystal-clear, glass case. Victoria's eyes grew wide when she saw the contents. She thought, *If only I could reach in and touch it!*

Inside the display case, Vickie saw blue, crushed velvet with the most incredibly shiny crown sitting on exhibit. Victoria had wanted a real tiara since she was a young girl. Of course, she had plastic ones back then, but ever since then she had yearned for a golden tiara like the one perched in front of her. Lights shone on the solid gold crown adorned with sparkling onyx, emeralds, rubies, and diamonds. The sight of it took her breath away. Vickie jumped up and down, clapping with excitement, while exclaiming, "I want that! Is it for me?"

"It was," the Voice said sadly. "God wanted to give you the gift of salvation, the *crown of life.*"

"Okay, I'll take it," Vickie said like a giddy little girl.

"Precious Child, it's too late. God didn't want you to perish and miss your chance of living forever with Him in Heaven, but your time is up and you clearly denied Him."

"See, that's not fair either," she pouted. "He only gave me twenty-seven years—I was going to look into this whole god-thing and religion when I got older."

Silence fell over the room. Standing alone in the empty area, Vickie started to feel nauseous. Her stomach was turning from the mixture of drugs and alcohol. Plus, she was feeling claustrophobic from the sight of the treasures taunting her. It was as if she was a child again, standing in a candy store and being told she couldn't have any sweets.

"Fine! I've had enough of this joint, and I've had enough of your god mumbo jumbo. Get me out of here, now!" she commanded, tapping the tip of her shoe annoyingly.

Vickie stood with her nose in the air, watching the door at the other end of the room slide open. In her stubborn pride, she stomped out of the colorful room, leaving God's unopened, unclaimed gifts behind, and headed back toward the *holding area.*

Chapter 11
Death and Dying

While Teresa and the others made their way from the *room of gifts* back to the *holding area,* Teresa's sixteen-year-old daughter, Lupita, was lying in a hospital bed on Earth, recovering from a head injury caused by the accident she, her mother, and her little sister had been in earlier that morning.

Lupita's eyes started to flutter in that way eyes do when one is trying to wake up. Her body felt heavy, as if she had been asleep for a very long time, yet judging by the blurry numbers on the clock on the wall in front of her, she had only been out of it half a day.

She startled to full consciousness when her eyes finally refocused. Looking up, she saw the visions of four faces staring down at her from their positions around the bed. She let out a small scream, jerked up on her elbows, and scanned her surroundings more thoroughly, desperate to see where she was and who the strangers were.

"Lupita, calm down," said one of the strangers dressed in colorful scrubs. Since it wasn't blatantly obvious what her job in the hospital was, she introduced herself. "Hello, Lupita. I am Irene, your nurse. You are in a hospital because you were in a horrible accident this morning. Do you remember your van being hit by a truck?" she asked, reaching up to check the flow of her patient's IV.

Lupita put her hand to her aching head and lay back down. It hurt to think, but she knew something serious had happened and that she needed to remember what it was. After a few minutes, she remembered a few details of the truck smashing into the van, but most of it was foggy.

"Oh, my head hurts," she said, "but I'll try to remember." She closed her eyes, tried to focus her thoughts on the events of earlier that morning, and then stated, "I was texting my friend, Maddie, when all of a sudden the van died. Mama was trying to get it started, when I looked down to text Maddie that I might be late for school. The next thing I remember was looking up and seeing a truck heading toward my sister's side of the van. It was going so fast; it didn't even try to avoid us."

By now, Lupita was sobbing. Recalling the hard pounding jolt that sent her younger sister, Angelica, smashing into her mother's seat in front of her, and then somewhere else in the twisted mass of steel as the van rolled was not something she wanted to do. She couldn't see Angelica's body once the van came to a stop—only traces of her baby sister's blood.

"Where's my mom and my sister?" she finally asked, scouring the room for any sign of them.

"Let's get you a glass of water," offered the second woman nervously. She was a strange looking, flamboyant lady with bright red hair and even brighter colored clothing. Lupita didn't know it yet, but the state had assigned this woman as a foster mother to her. Seeing how upset the young girl was, the heavyset woman tried to distract Lupita from asking too many questions.

"Who are you?" Lupita asked, confused as to why this woman was here trying to soothe and take care of her instead of her mother.

"I'm Rosie, your new friend," the chubby woman who appeared to be around sixty years old answered.

I don't really need new friends right now, thought Lupita. *I just want my family*. But instead of asking for them again, she asked, "Who's that guy and the little girl?" She pointed at the two other strangers standing just behind Rosie.

Rosie reached for them and put her arms around the boy, introducing him as her foster son, and then she did the same with her foster daughter. "Steven is eighteen," Rosie added, "but he's a little slow, so he's more like a twelve-year-old. And little Cindi is ten."

"Okay?" Lupita said sarcastically frowning, still confused by the whole situation. "Nice to meet you all. Now, why isn't anyone answering my question about my family?" She looked up at the three people and the nurse she had just met who were standing around her hospital bed and noticed the looks of trepidation on all four faces.

"Are you keeping something from me? Did something happen to them?" she asked the strangers. She could sense the hysteria in her voice and feel her heart beating so hard and fast in her chest that the tissue and muscles around it felt sore and bruised. Tears were threatening to spill over, and her breaths were starting to come in short, rapid bursts.

"Where are they?" Lupita shouted. She began to shake uncontrollably, and then she screamed, "Why isn't someone answering me?"

In order to calm Lupita down, nurse Irene ushered Rosie and the two kids out of the hospital room. Rosie wished the children hadn't seen their new foster sister so upset, but she hadn't been able to find a baby sitter to watch them. When the phone rang early that morning saying a young girl was in the hospital and needed her, Rosie had dropped everything and rushed to her side.

Inside her room, the nurse quickly returned to Lupita's bedside. Irene gently and lovingly grabbed the young teen's hand, looked caringly into her eyes, and tenderly said, "Lay back, Lupita. Calm down, and I will explain."

The kind nurse adjusted the hospital bed and then helped her patient fluff her pillows into a comfortable position. "You were in a terrible car accident, as you know. Your mother was driving; you and your sister were in the backseat. The van died in the middle of a busy intersection, and, because the driver of the other vehicle didn't see you in time, his truck slammed into yours. The force of the impact sent your mother's van flipping and rolling. Do you recall any of that?"

"It's starting to come back to me," Lupita said, trying to slow her breathing down, using the calming breathing techniques her instructor taught in her Yoga classes. "Were they hurt…you know, my mom and my sister?"

"I'm afraid so," answered nurse Irene cautiously. "I'm very sorry to inform you that they didn't make it."

Lupita's eyes went wide as saucers, and her mouth opened with a scream, "That can't be! You're lying to me!" She tried to jerk back the hospital blankets and pull at the needles and tubes running to her body from the various machines that had been monitoring her since she was brought into the hospital, but her movements were wild and uncoordinated, plus she was weaker and more tired than she realized.

The kind nurse reached out, swept Lupita into her arms, and held her tightly to her chest. "I'm so sorry, Sweetie," she said over and over, as the two rocked back and forth. Lupita quickly gave up the fight and let the woman hold her, to comfort her aching heart.

The next morning, Rosie left her other foster kids with her neighbor so that she could return to the hospital. She entered Lupita's room with brightly colored tulips in her hands.

"Hi, sleepy head. I was hoping these flowers would cheer you up. I realize you've been through a terrible ordeal—this must be a really tough time for you," she said, rambling a bit nervously as she fluttered around the room, placing the vase on the stand next to Lupita and moving random objects around in a nervous need to do something.

The dark-haired beauty was already awake and, by the look in her eyes, she was feeling sad and depressed. "No kidding!" Lupita muttered, obviously wishing Rosie would go away and leave her alone. Rosie knew that nothing was going to cheer the girl up, not now, not ever.

"Did you get any sleep?" Rosie asked, though it was obvious she hadn't.

Lupita only shook her head from side to side. No, she hadn't been able to sleep the night before, which made her tired and irritable. The annoyingly loud sounds of the busy hospital unit had kept her awake. The constant beeping of her heart rate and blood pressure monitors made her feel a little crazy. She wanted to reach over and switch them off.

While she had laid there in her hospital bed listening to the soft voices of nurses moving around in the hall, and the disparaging moans and cries from the patient sharing the room with her, she thought about her life and realized she was now alone in the world. Both sets of her grandparents were gone. Her only living aunt and uncle resided in care facilities due to serious health problems, and who knew where her father lived. Moreover, who would want to live with such a mean, abusive man anyway!

Each time Roberto had hit Lupita in the past and thrown her against the wall, she forgave him. She gave him second chance after second chance, because she believed him when he said he would change. As she grew into her teen years, though, she began to struggle with unforgiveness and bitterness toward her father. *How could he love liquor more than his own daughter?* she had wondered. *How could he leave us? He was supposed to be the man of the house.* Rosie heard her sigh loudly and came quickly to her side.

"Lupita, I realize you are probably feeling alone and fearful, and that's why I am here. I have been assigned to be your foster mother," Rosie informed her.

"I don't need another mother," Lupita blurted out. "I just need *my* mom back!" she shouted, before turning her head into her pillow, letting it absorb her tears.

"I know, Chica…I know," Rosie said, while running her hand soothingly up and down Lupita's arm as she cried.

"I just want to die!" Lupita finally said once her tears had slowed. She turned her head slightly, still sniffling to look at the woman. "Why didn't God take me too? Why did he take them away from me? Angel was my best friend, and my mother took good care of us." Talking about her mother and sister in the past tense brought on a new round of sobs.

"We didn't have a lot, but she always made us feel loved. I thought that God loved us too, but now I hate him!" she shouted, slamming her fist into the hospital mattress in the only gesture of anger she had the energy to show at that moment.

"Pita," Rosie said, taking a chance that shortening the girl's name to a nickname might help Lupita warm up to her. Touching her arm tenderly, she continued. "You mustn't say such things. God does love you, and He must have other plans for you. It just wasn't your time to go yet," Rosie admonished.

"I don't care what you say. He's mean!" Lupita jerked her arm from the woman's touch and turned her back to her, signaling that she had nothing more to say.

Rosie could see Lupita was in no mood to be consoled. She understood how the young girl felt; her parents also died in a car accident when she was seventeen—Rosie had been visiting her cousins in Mexico when it happened. She would never forget the look on her uncle's face when he told her what had happened. Rosie fell apart after hearing the life-changing, horrific news.

She recalled being so upset that she had to be given a shot to calm her down, and then sleeping pills and antidepressants to help her traverse the momentous hurdles of her parents' funerals, sorting through their personal items, and then selling her childhood home. Rosie also recalled crying incessantly back then, not being able to sleep those first couple months, and going through her days in a sort of cloudy haze.

Because she shared the commonality of grief with Lupita, she felt deep compassion for the young orphan. Knowing there was nothing more she could say to her, she decided to give the girl some time to herself, so she left her bedside to look for nurse Irene. Recognizing the woman's flaming red hair in the hallway, the nurse, who happened to be standing nearby at the nurse's station, turned around and greeted Rosie.

"The doctors are going to be running more tests on your foster daughter this afternoon to determine the extent of her brain injury," the nurse reported. "They say it doesn't appear there's a great deal of swelling, so she's got that going for her."

Suddenly, there was a loud commotion coming from the direction of Lupita's room. Both women immediately turned and ran around the corner to the teenager's bedside. Nurse Irene took over once she saw that Lupita was convulsing. Rosie backed out of the way while the nurse alerted other staff members to call the doctor-on-charge, since it appeared that Lupita was having a seizure.

The doctor and a few other nurses ran into the room; they were aware of Lupita's accident and subsequent head trauma. Because she had only been in the hospital overnight, they had only run a few tests thus far, so they didn't know the severity of her injuries yet.

Lupita was shaking violently in her bed; her head flopped around, and she was not coherent, nor was she able to control her bodily functions. After a few minutes, the thrashing of her limbs slowed, and then Lupita vomited, causing the nurses to rush and check her airway to make sure she didn't choke on any of the fluids protruding from her mouth.

The doctor looked around and noticed Rosie standing in the corner. He began shooting rapid-fire questions at her before she could answer them: "What was this girl like before the accident? Did she experience any form of mental confusion the days before the wreck? Has she experienced seizures or convulsions in the past?"

He was staring at her for answers, when Rosie finally spoke up. "I...I...I just met her. I was only assigned as her foster mother yesterday."

"Were you speaking with her before the seizure?" the doctor asked rapidly.

"Yes, she seemed fine. She shared about the accident a little bit."

He rushed her by interjecting, "Did she vomit, or complain of nausea or a headache?"

"She said her head hurt," Rosie answered.

The doctor turned away and asked nurse Irene if the results for the CT scan they did on Lupita earlier that morning were back yet. She left the room to find out. He then asked the other nurses for her blood pressure, and then he ordered them to start Lupita on oxygen.

The studious looking, tall, thin doctor turned his attention back to Rosie. He took his glasses off and rubbed his eyes. Rosie wondered when he had last slept. Putting his glasses back in place, he told her, "The CT scan will tell us a lot about what's going on here. Sometimes people have little or no obvious signs of trauma at first, and then episodes such as this occur.

"I'm concerned that Lupita might have a depressed skull fracture, which means part of the bone is pressing on or into her skull. If that is the case, she'll have to go to surgery this afternoon. I am also worried about her possibly having an acute subdural hematoma. That means a collection of blood..."

"Doctor," interrupted one of the nurses at Lupita's side, "she's unconscious."

"That's what I was afraid of," he said to the nurse. He then turned to Rosie and stated regretfully, "It appears she has slipped into a coma."

"Let's get her moved over to ICU stat!" he ordered the nurses.

Rosie's hand covered her mouth. She was shocked at how quickly the teenager had gone from awake and talking to lying in front of her in a coma.

Rosie followed as the medical personnel moved Lupita's bed out into the hallway. They were moving her to the ICU when her cell phone rang. The person on the other end was her neighbor, who informed her that she needed to get to a dental appointment she had forgotten about, so Rosie needed to pick up Steven and Cindi.

"I can't leave my new foster daughter now. They are moving her to the ICU. It's important that I stay with her," she told her neighbor. Thankfully, the woman was kind enough to offer to drop the kids off at the hospital on her way to the dentist.

Once they arrived, Rosie took both kids to the ICU to visit Lupita. At first, the nurses wouldn't allow her to take Cindi into the room, because she was underage, but Rosie explained that she couldn't leave a ten-year-old loitering alone in the halls or waiting room, so they changed their minds and allowed Cindi a brief visit.

When she entered the room, Cindi walked over and stared at Lupita's pale-looking face.

"Is she dead, Rosie?" the little girl inquired.

"No, Honey," she answered, walking over and standing next to the young child. "Lupita is only sleeping."

"Do you think she will like this daisy?" Cindi asked innocently. She laid the wilted dandelion she had picked from Rosie's neighbor's lawn on the bed next to Lupita's arm. Cindi had never mentioned it to Rosie, but the little girl had wanted a big sister very badly. On more than one occasion, Rosie had overheard Cindi pretending to have a big sister. She and the pretend sister went shopping together, played board games, and did each other's hair and nails.

Steven walked over and stared at Lupita, too.

"Pita is pretty," he told Rosie bashfully. She noticed he was smiling, blushing, and rocking back and forth, indicating he was feeling shy. "Rosie," he confided, "I don't want another foster sister, I want a girlfriend."

Rosie looked at the young man half-irritated. She didn't want him hurting Cindi's feelings, plus it didn't appear to be the time or place to be having this conversation.

Not waiting for her response, Steven continued in a sweet, loving manner. "I would treat her tenderly and gently, like she was a fragile piece of glass. I would hold her and protect her and keep her safe."

From the way he looked at her, Rosie could tell Steven thought Pita was the prettiest girl he had ever seen. She wondered if it was love at first sight for the young boy.

"If she loves me back, I will be the happiest person in the whole wide world," Steven finished.

Rosie was in no mood to deal with puppy love, so she walked over near the window and sat down in a chair to rest her weary eyes instead.

After about ten minutes, Lupita's new nurse, Janet, who had been watching her patient and checking her vital signs regularly, told Rosie that Cindi's visit was now over. Rosie stood to escort the fifth grader back to the hospital's sterile waiting area, while Steven stayed with Lupita. Sitting on a chair next to her bed, he leaned down and placed his head on her stomach. Nurse Janet thought it was a touching sight. She didn't know this new family's story and she thought Steven was the girl's brother or boyfriend.

Nurse Janet continued staying with Lupita as well, paying careful attention to her vital signs and making sure her oxygen levels were normal.

While Lupita lay sleeping, she had recurring dreams. One of her dreams that seemed to play back over and over was about her adventures in Heaven with her sister, her Nana, her Uncle Richard, and her mother. She pictured the five of them enjoying every benefit of their heavenly existence. In her visions, their bodies were stronger and more attractive than the ones they had on Earth. The Heaven she pictured them in was circular with different quadrants.

One was for dessert lovers; it was unique because the residents could eat as much as they wanted and never gain an ounce. Everywhere she looked there were crystal displays containing glass shelves arranged with oatmeal cookies, chocolate chip cupcakes with whipped cream icing, strawberry rhubarb pies, and pumpkin bread—all of her favorites. The aroma filled the air with sweet richness.

Another quadrant was like a large 777 screen cinema. Clean-cut, wholesome movies were playing everywhere for each personality's particular preference, and she could smell the scent of buttered popcorn wafting through the air. Since it was Lupita's version of Heaven, she made sure all of the movies had happy endings.

In her heavenly quarters, no one worked, had chores, or homework to do. Instead, chubby faced angels with fluffy wings catered to all the needs of Heaven's inhabitants, including cooking, cleaning, changing litter boxes, gardening, and other things Lupita didn't like to do.

Another quadrant in Lupita's dream contained lounge chairs where people sat and listened to worship music. It was a place of calm and tranquility. People closed their eyes and hummed along to their favorite tunes while losing themselves in the pleasing melodies.

Bella, Lupita's gray and white cat, was in the pet lovers' quadrant. There were dogs, birds, and other pets there as well. They purred and barked, parrots talked, and none of the animals bit or scratched. They loved being petted and played with; hence, children spent lots of time there.

In the middle of the circular Heaven Lupita envisioned were stairs leading up to God. In her version of Heaven, he was a loving daddy. Anyone could go to Him anytime and sit on His lap. The stairs leading to Him were always covered with bodies lying at His feet. He was always available, and never, ever too tired, grumpy, or irritated to listen. It was obvious that He loved nothing more than spending time with Heaven's residents, and Lupita was usually the first in line.

She could clearly picture the Heaven she looked forward to. It was easy for her to visualize herself interacting with her newfound Kingdom family. Everyone was kind and generous. Their motives were pure and righteous—she didn't have to fear anyone taking advantage of her, or having someone stab her in the back as she had experienced on Earth. Relationships were unblemished by hidden motives, ridicule, or manipulation like what she had experienced with her father.

While Pita lay sleeping in her hospital bed, she could almost feel the heavenly love she dreamt of wrapping around her like a warm blanket on a cold day.

Unbeknownst to her, Steven remained next to her side for seven hours, contently watching her sleep. Lupita seemed perfectly normal to him—she yawned a couple times, she swallowed, and she even opened her eyes once, but she wouldn't talk to him. Steven was confused and asked the nurse why Lupita was ignoring him.

"Honey," said nurse Janet, "your friend is in a persistent vegetative state. That means she will be asleep for a very long time, but her body will perform normal functions now and then." Steven didn't understand, but it didn't matter to him. He was content holding the pretty, young teen's soft hand.

Chapter 12
Last Breath

Again, alarms went off and red lights flickered in the *holding area*. Lupita Hernandez walked through Earth's passageway and into section 9:02 p.m. A glorious angel had lifted her from the hospital bed and told her she was going on a journey. While floating upward, she looked back down and saw Steven, the boy she had met earlier that day, sitting next to her sleeping body. She couldn't imagine how she could be flying upward with the angel, when she could clearly see herself lying in the hospital bed below. Pita was perplexed, yet exhilarated, at the same time about the adventure she was going on.

Still wearing her light gray hospital gown and her mind groggy, she shyly entered the *holding area*. This time, when she refocused her eyes, there were even more strangers staring at her—lots of strangers!

She looked around in total confusion. Questions flooded her mind. *Where is my hospital bed? Why did the angel bring me to this strange place?* Lupita didn't know it, but her heart had stopped, and, before the hospital personnel could get to her, the angel entered her room to escort her through the passageway leading to section 9:02 p.m. of the *holding area.*

She turned to a kind looking man standing next to her and tried asking him where she was, but he didn't speak English or Spanish. He shook his head, and lifted his hands to show her that he didn't understand her question.

A soft calming Voice then spoke, saying, "Lupita, do not be afraid." Of course, she couldn't help her feelings of anxiety and fear. She was all alone in a strange place, not to mention she suspected she was hearing things. She bent her neck to look upward, but, seeing no speakers, she realized she must be having another dream, like the one she had the night before about being in Heaven with her loved ones. She hoped she would fall back to sleep soon, so she could jump back into that wonderful version of Heaven.

"Lupita Dawn Hernandez," the Voice continued, tenderly and unthreateningly, "I, the Lord of the Universe, have allowed you to come here because I have a message for you."

Lupita was in shock at what she was hearing. Her eyes searched the area, hoping one of the strangers around her would walk up and tell her what was going on. She wasn't sure if she believed in God, plus she was only sixteen and didn't expect to meet Him until she was around eighty years old, or so. Before she could ask if she had died, the Voice spoke again.

"I know all about you, precious daughter—I knew you before the Earth and all its inhabitants were created. Your name refers to my earthly mother, Mary. You have 108,671 hairs on your beautiful head. You have cried half-a-pint of tears in your lifetime. Yes, I know you well, and I understand your fears, sweet daughter."

Lupita felt as if her mouth had dropped to the floor. She could hardly believe her ears. She thought either what she was experiencing was an illusion, or the Voice she was hearing really was God's. No one could know that kind of information about her, except for a supreme being. Only one Being could have counted the hairs on her head. She recalled Nana telling her a Bible verse about that. She also remembered a verse out of Psalms saying that God keeps track of the tears human beings shed.

"God?" she mumbled under her breath. "Are you telling me I am actually speaking to God?" she asked skeptically.

"Yes, my beloved, I am God the Father, the Daddy you dreamed of earlier today."

Lupita almost fainted. *Only the Lord could know my thoughts.* Once she composed herself, Pita asked, "Okay, then, does that mean I am dead, or am I dreaming that I am dead?"

While waiting for an answer, she glanced around to see the deformed and broken bodies standing and sitting around her. See noticed some people looked deathly ill, others had blood-soaked clothing, and some were missing body parts. It was all starting to make sense to her.

"Your time on Earth is very short, Pita. It is critical, my darling, that you examine your heart and determine your feelings for me. Until now, I have been knocking at the door of your heart, and you have turned the knob, but you haven't fully opened the door and allowed me in. I am a gentleman; I will not knock the door down and force myself on you against your will."

The shocked teen was drawn to the love she was feeling for this Being who was wooing her with what appeared to be pure, righteous motives. She had never been in love before, until now. She felt like the most special person ever born—

she hadn't felt cherished since she was a small child sitting on Nana's lap. Hearing that the mighty God of the Universe was so in tune with a peon like her was overwhelming. Tears of joy and gratitude streaked down her cheeks.

"I'm so sorry I was angry with you, Lord. Please forgive me for being so upset, and for saying I hated you. I don't, I really don't! I love you! Please forgive me!" she begged, now on her knees sobbing uncontrollably.

Between sobs, Lupita tried to talk. "My mother and sister were killed—well, I guess you already know that. I was scared. I didn't mean to say I hated you. It was a stupid thing to say." Lupita found herself babbling, so she shut up and waited for some kind of instruction from the kind King.

"Lupita, stand up my dear." She did while the Voice continued. "Let me explain how special you are to me. I will not hold your honest venting against you. I realize that losing your family was incredibly hard for you to bear. That's why I sent people to help you with your grief and mourning. I never intended to hurt you, yet it was your mother and sister's time to leave Earth.

"I understand that you are not sure about your feelings for me, but know this: I am always with you, and I will never, ever depart from you. Some people fear that while I am providing for millions of people's needs, and keeping the entire solar system spinning in perfect harmony, I will be too busy to hear when they call. This is not true. I do not have human limitations. I am not three-dimensional. You are free to dump all of your problems, anxieties, and fears on me. I can withstand it."

Tears continued gushing down her cheeks while Lupita listened. These were the kind of words she wished her earthly father had said to her. Now, in reality, her eternal Father was saying them, and it touched her heart deeply.

"Remember," the Voice continued, "I am never too busy to listen to you. I don't fall asleep and miss your calls, and I never tire of hearing your prayers. I will never put you on hold so that I can listen to someone else. You are near and dear to my heart, and I long for you to return my love for you."

Lupita couldn't have been happier. She felt as if she had just met the Daddy in her dream about Heaven that she had while in a coma—the one at the top of the stairs who was always available, and never, ever, too tired, grumpy, or irritated to listen.

There was a moment of silence; Lupita contemplated what she was undergoing and the reality of what she was hearing. The words she heard earlier suddenly sunk in. *He said my time is short. Does that mean I'm dying soon?* she wondered.

Finally, she asked, "Can I see you face to face? I don't know what to do next. What do you want me to do? Please tell me."

"Dear one, what I want you to do is turn around and look through the glass."

Lupita wiped the tears from her face and slowly turned around. She had no idea what to expect. So far, she could have never imagined what she was experiencing. Looking ahead, Lupita noticed there was a crowd of people in front of her who seemed fascinated by something. She made her way to the front of the crowd and then gasped at the resplendent sight laid out in front of her.

"Is that Heaven?" she yelled out excitedly to everyone within listening distance. Everyone in section 9:02 p.m. were flabbergasted at the prospect of utopia. "It's exquisite!" she added in dismay. "It reminds me of the Garden of Eden my Nana used to read to me about!"

The Voice spoke again. "Yes it is, Lupita, my dear. Now look closer."

She started jumping up and down when she spotted her sister Angelica, her Uncle Richard, and her Nana. Waving her hands in the air, she screamed, "Angelica, it's me, Pita!" She tapped on the glass, and repeated, "Angel, I'm over here!"

"Lupita," the Voice announced, "they can't hear you."

"What?" she said deflated. "I don't understand."

"Lupita, your departed loved ones are on the other side— in the place I have prepared for them."

Her mouth opened wide as she contemplated what was going on.

"So, you *are* saying they are in Heaven, right? I hope so, because that Heaven is even better than the one I imagined in my dream!" she shouted in amazement, looking through the glass.

"Pita, I created Heaven for those who love Me and accept Me. That is why I am allowing you to see your loved ones. They accepted My invitation. I dearly want *you* to accept My invitation to a heavenly residence soon."

"But, I don't see my mother!" Lupita said disappointedly.

"Dear one, I loved your mother as much as I love you; however, she couldn't find it in her heart to believe in me."

God didn't tell Lupita that Teresa was in a section of the *holding area* just ahead of hers on her way to her final judgment. Because He is omnipresent, Lupita's mother was having conversations with Him at the same time she was.

Lupita was quiet, her feelings of nirvana abruptly weighed down by sadness. Memories filled her mind of Teresa's hostility toward organized religion. She remembered her mother saying that God was make-believe. She had also told her daughters she didn't have to worship somebody to feel good about herself.

Oh, no, thought Lupita. Her stomach began to turn, and she felt nervous when she recalled her mother mentioning several times that she didn't want anyone owning her soul but herself.

"God, Mama was a good person. I want her in Heaven with me!"

Of course, God knew Lupita's worries and concerns. "That was up to her, dear one. You couldn't make that decision for her," the Voice said calmly.

Lupita was noticeably disappointed and sad. Tears exploded down her cheeks again, once she realized she would never see her madre again.

"Lord, I'm feeling angry again. I'm sorry—I can't lie about my feelings, because you know me so well. I'm upset, because I wanted our whole family in Heaven together."

"I understand, Pita, that's a natural response. However, I made myself known to her, I blessed your mother, and I showed her love and acceptance in more ways than your human mind can comprehend."

In her heart of hearts, Lupita knew it was true. "I think that Mama was so angry and hurt about the pain she experienced from her father and then my Dad that she convinced herself she didn't deserve anything better."

"I am sad, too, Precious One," the Voice said glumly. "I could not, and would not, force your mother to accept me. That is each person's private decision to make."

At such a young age, it was difficult for Lupita to understand God's ways. She had always declared herself an agnostic; therefore, she dabbled in several belief systems, and she entertained the thoughts of different godheads.

But once she had glimpsed upon her loving Father God and His heavenly Kingdom, she knew her life had changed forever. She now realized how big God's love was, and that it wasn't about religion. Even though she was disappointed about her mother's fate, what mattered most to her now was whether her heart was vacant or occupied by the Spirit of the Lord God. She chose the latter.

Chapter 13
Welcome Home

By now, Teresa had returned to the *holding area* from the *room of gifts*. She had no idea that Lupita was in one of the sections located behind her. If she had known, she would have been at the glass partition scouring all the sections she could see behind her until she found her baby girl. What a relief it would have been for her to see Lupita's face again.

Instead, Teresa was feeling distraught after seeing a room full of gifts intended for her, yet left unopened. She understood now how gifts from God were her strengths, abilities, and talents. She could see how he had gifted her with organizational skills, leadership capabilities, as well as the gift of hospitality.

Teresa wished she had been more open to the whole *God concept* while she was alive. Perhaps she would have taken advantage of the many gifts she saw sitting on the shelves in the other room, such as the gifts of mercy, giving, and helping others. Then, perhaps she would have been less self-absorbed in her own problems.

Sighing heavily, Teresa sat down next to a man who was staring out the glass at the bright lights of Heaven. Because he was holding his face in his hands, she guessed he was probably feeling nostalgic as well. Looking over at her, the gentleman introduced himself as Reuben, and then began speaking.

"Do you see the Great High Priest over there?" he asked her in Spanish. Thankfully, Teresa understood, even though his dialect was a bit different from hers. She didn't feel like getting into a theological debate with the stranger, so she merely nodded her head up and down.

"He gave me many gifts to use for His glory, but I was foolish," the man said, looking at Teresa as if she had known him for a long time. "I thought my material possessions were a sign of God's blessings on me. I became rich and arrogant. Earthly wealth, luxuries, and possessions made me feel satisfied and proud, yet I became complacent. Looking back, I didn't even realize how I hoarded the gifts I received."

Teresa was surprised that the complete stranger was spilling his guts to her.

"I became cynical and critical, afraid that everyone was after my money. Now I realize those possessions and achievements were worthless without God in my life. All of my money and fancy things are back home. I don't have a dollar to my name," he said sadly, pulling his empty pants pockets out for her to see.

Teresa thought for a while and then asked, "What did you do to accumulate such wealth?"

Reuben lowered his head and remained silent for a while. He then cocked his head to the side, half-looking at Teresa, and spoke slowly, as if he were forcing himself to spit the words out.

"I've never told anyone this, but I created a bogus charity. I led unsuspecting people in my country to believe their donations would feed starving children all over Central America, in countries such as El Salvador, Honduras, Guatemala...but I kept the majority of the money."

Looking at her further, he saw the look of astonishment on Teresa's face, so he quickly interceded. "I felt guilty at first, but when I realized all the things I could do...like traveling to countries I've always wanted to see, and buying my wife the kind of clothes and jewelry I thought she deserved..." Reuben stopped speaking. The words sounded ludicrous once he actually heard them out loud.

Teresa remembered seeing something about a scam in El Salvador on the news a few days earlier, and that the founder had a heart attack and was in critical condition.

Without waiting for a response from her, Reuben got on his knees, joining so many others around Teresa who had knelt in supplication, and were lifting their tear-stained faces to the God of love they were witnessing first hand in hopes that He would somehow have mercy on them. Some bowed and prayed in reverence, while others cried in fear of what lay ahead for them. None of them knew yet that it was too late to beg for salvation.

Teresa and those around her were lost in their thoughts as their section moved effortlessly down the corridor. Even though none of them knew where they were going next, the majority hoped to join the people on the other side of the glass. Looking ahead, they saw what appeared to be a homecoming celebration or reunion going on over there, and each person yearned to be part of it. They spent hours watching through the glass—it was like seeing a great movie and guessing what the characters would do next.

While those huddled around the immense window continued observing, the multitudes of Heaven had stopped what
they were doing and made their way over to greet and welcome the Holy City's newest tenant. There were lines of souls
waiting to celebrate a man's entrance into his new heavenly
residence.

A blonde-haired woman, who had been kneeling with the
man named Reuben, stood up. She could see that the group
of people crowded around the glass was curious to know
about this stranger on the other side. Looking out the large
pane, she informed them that she could read lips. The blonde
watched the movements of the man's lips on the other side
for a few seconds, and then she said that from what she could
see, it appeared his name was Nikolai Koslauvsky or Kozlowski (actually, it turned out to be the latter spelling). Teresa and the others watching couldn't help but wonder what
kind of life he had led on Earth.

Maxine, the busybody, walked over next to the glass and
stood between Reuben and Teresa. Just the sight of the med-
dlesome woman made Teresa feel tense and agitated. Her
shoulders stiffened, and she felt her teeth clenching immediately.

Upon seeing Nikolai at the gates of Heaven, Maxine
thought for a while, and then finally spoke up, saying, "I bet
that guy over there is Russian."

"What makes you think that?" Teresa asked, clearly annoyed by the older woman's know-it-all attitude.

"He's got that square Russian jaw I've always loved!" Maxine answered, smiling for the first time since entering the *holding area*.

"Let me see," she said, holding her own jaw in her liver-
spotted hand, "I bet he was married and had three kids...no,

make that two kids—both handsome, rugged boys. Hum..."
She thought for a few minutes. "He probably worked in the
steel industry and..."

"No, Maxine, that's not even close," Herb, the pilot, interrupted dogmatically. He had heard her comments while walking by, so he stopped and looked at the Kingdom's next resident. He had a completely different rendition of the man's
past on the other side of the glass. People in the area watched
while the two German-speaking souls bantered back and
forth over who was right about the man's previous life.

Actually, neither one of them came close to guessing the
man's true-life story. Originally from Poland, Nikolai Kozlowski was a despised man when he lived on Earth. He
moved to America when he was eighteen years old, and became a career criminal. Most of his years he spent in and out
of prison.

Still living in Poland, Nikolai's parents received updates
from him each time he was in jail, but the letters were hostile
and upsetting. They wondered what they did wrong to rear
such an evil man. Both his mother and father had basically
given up on him until one day when, out of the blue, both felt
a deep conviction to pray for their son. They had no idea
why, but they insisted that all of their friends and relatives
pray for him as well.

Nikolai had been on death row, and, unbeknownst to his
parents, a date had been set for his execution. Once he knew
he was surely going to die, Nikolai had called a local priest to
visit him at the prison. The older gentleman held mass with
the prisoners every Sunday evening at the penitentiary, so Father Mike was familiar with the institution.

Nikolai met the tall, dark-haired, Italian man in the commons area, where he explained the reason for his visit. Father Mike was familiar with the gloomy room and sat down on a lopsided metal chair to talk.

"Father, I've squandered twenty-seven years of my life in here," Nikolai said. "I've been playing a game of 'get them before they get me.' I constantly fear having a physical altercation or a confrontation with the officers, so I've tried to put on a façade that I am greater than them…mightier and even more powerful. My goal has been for them to fear me, but, in actuality, I'm scared all the time." It was clear to Father Mike by the look on the prisoner's face that he was being real with him.

"Sometimes, I purposely get into trouble so I can hide out in the hole," Nikolai continued. "When I'm alone in there, it hurts to realize I will never have a family or live a normal life as far as marriage and children are concerned. I will never be an integral part of a community or spend quality time with my loved ones.

"As much as I've hurt those around me, I think the person I've let down the most is myself. I was such a fool to believe that life was all about me…how I could party the most…who I could use to get what I wanted. Father, I've hurt so many people on the outside physically and emotionally—my parents, my ex-girlfriend, family members, and friends in the little town I grew up in, in Poland. That list doesn't even include those I have intentionally hurt or abandoned here in America.

"To make things worse, I've had to earn the other prisoners' respect to make it in here—I couldn't show fear. But truth be known, I'm afraid of dying," he said softly, so that no one around them would hear the truth of how he felt.

The priest had been forewarned that Nikolai was going to be executed by lethal injection soon, so he listened while the prisoner continued. "I pretended to be a Satanist in here, but it was an act to keep myself alive. Father, if I prayed to God, would He hear from such an evil man as me?"

"Yes," the priest said, tenderly nodding his head up and down. "He's been waiting to hear from you for a lifetime. He's never, ever given up on you."

Nikolai fought back the tears while asking the Italian priest to pray with him. "I want to go to Heaven, Father. Will God allow me in after all I've done?"

"Yes," the pontiff replied with a subtle Italian inflection. "Jesus is the way, the truth, and the life; no one comes to the Father except through Him. Once you die, you will go one of two places. To go to Heaven, you need a Savior to pay the penalty for your sins because redemption isn't free; however, the gift of eternal life is. Do you believe Christ died for you?" Father Mike asked. Nikolai agreed that Jesus freely gave up His life to pay the ransom for his transgressions.

The priest asked Nikolai to bow his head and pray along with him. The prisoner lowered his head, closed his eyes, and allowed Father Mike to pray over him. The friar prayed that God would find favor on Nikolai and absolve him of his sins. He continued to pray that the Lord would bless the new believer with eternal life.

When Nikolai opened his eyes and lifted his head, he felt victorious—as if he was starting a fresh, new life. Father Mike continued, saying, "Now, I want you to spend the next three months living a changed life. Write the people you've hurt and ask forgiveness. In turn, forgive those who have trespassed against you. Serve others, pray, and read this Bible."

He handed a simple looking, black, leather-bound book to the new believer.

From that day forward, Nikolai was a new person. He did as the priest had counseled him to do; he went to mass every Sunday, and he read his Bible out in the open—something not accepted by the other inmates. On his cellblock, it was an unspoken rule that religion was off limits. If one of the prisoners lived their faith outwardly, they were basically making themselves a target for ridicule, hostility, or even death. Nikolai knew the other prisoners wanted to kill him even before his conversion, but now he didn't care. He was going to be a light in the darkness, no matter what.

The other inmates were shocked at the change in Nikolai. Word traveled quickly that the once satanic leader had become an overnight Jesus freak. Some thought he was hiding behind his faith, others thought he was a hypocrite. Before, he had been a force to be reckoned with—a very large, vile, angry man who eagerly looked for opportunities to inflict harm on the other lifers. Now, he was a giant teddy bear.

Don't get me wrong, life wasn't easy for Nikolai over the next ninety-one days. The prisoners he had picked on, or hurt, in the past came to inflict revenge on him. They trapped him in enclosed areas such as the shower, exercise room, and the yard, and then beat him severely on several occasions. Being a large man, he endured it better than most, except when several of his worst enemies nearly hanged him by a cord one of the guys obtained from his girlfriend when she visited him.

Nevertheless, he kept his head held high—bruised cheekbones, eyelids, throat, fat lip, and all. He wasn't going to allow anyone to steal his joy. Even when he was in the yard, he sang praises to the Lord and recited verses aloud from his

Bible. Then he hoped and prayed someone else would find the courage to step out in faith someday. He would have been happy if just one person was saved from Hell because of his example.

Then on that fateful day, Nikolai heard the sounds of the boots of the prison guards echoing in the corridor as they finally arrived at his cell on death row to escort him to the execution chamber. Father Mike and a state-appointed chaplain were already in his cell, talking to him about the last minutes of his earthly life and what he could expect to see in the glorious realm of Heaven. Nikolai couldn't help but smile, knowing he was 100 percent confident of his eternal resting place due to his confession of faith.

He took off his orange T-shirt and blue pants, and dressed in the fresh pair the guards brought for him to wear, and then they connected him to an electrocardiogram heart monitor they had rolled into his cell on a cart when they first arrived. One of them then reported over a handheld radio that the inmate was ready. Once the guard heard from the voice on the other end, which belonged to the warden, to bring the prisoner to the execution chamber, the guards took Nikolai by each arm, escorting him out of his death-watch cell along with the priest and the chaplain.

Nikolai cooperated with them, while telling them about his testimony and conversion during the thousand-foot walk down the eerily quiet hallway. His voice echoed off the corridor walls, plus the cart carrying the EKG machine attached to him clanked noisily each time it hit a crack in the concrete floor. He listened intently to every clank, clank, clank, the wheels of the cart made. The guards remained quiet, wondering if the prisoner was telling them the truth or setting them up to believe he was something he wasn't. After all, they had seen it all when it came to human behavior.

Upon arriving at the execution chamber, the guards laid the tall, strong man on a gurney and secured his body to the table with six, strong, leather straps, and his ankles and wrists with lined restraints. Again, Nikolai cooperated completely, as his eye scoured the old-fashioned looking room. He wasn't upset with them—it wasn't their fault he was in this mess—he knew the blame was his to bear.

He wasn't going to fight them, either. Even though he had previously been afraid to die, he wasn't anymore. Nikolai was going to take it like a man. After all, he was banking on the Bible; it said that if he stepped out in childlike faith and believed that Christ died for his sins, God would consider him an heir to Heaven. Once he made the decision to commit himself to God's control, he no longer worried about his destiny.

Still able to lift his head, Nikolai again surveyed the chamber and saw two windows. He didn't realize it, but one was to an adjoining room that contained the toxic chemicals the team would inject him with. He surmised the other was probably for the witness room. Suddenly, he found himself wondering who was on the other side of the one-way mirror. He wasn't expecting his family to attend, and he wondered if people he had hurt during his infamous career came to watch him die. Laying his head back down and closing his eyes, he recounted with sadness the horrible choices that landed him in this place.

Pokes on both sides of his arms brought his attention back to the present, as he looked up and noticed a team of unfamiliar looking people inserting two IV tubes into veins in each of his arms. Nikolai flinched from the pain caused by the roughness of the needle pricks. Looking into the man's face on his left, he humbly stated, "I'm not an animal."

The man looked away, ignoring the comment, as he helped thread the intravenous tubes through an opening in the wall that lead to the attached room Nikolai noticed earlier. Because he couldn't see through the one-way mirror into the anteroom, he wasn't aware that's where the executioners were located.

Nikolai felt the saline solution beginning to flow into his arms, and he wondered if poison was already entering his system when a familiar looking man walked near him—it was the warden. He drew back a curtain from the one-way mirror on the wall to allow witnesses to view the execution, and then he looked over to Nikolai and asked, "Any last words?" rather apathetically while looking at the prisoner with disgust and disapproval.

Nikolai smiled broadly and then prayed out loud, thanking God for His mercy, His grace, and for forgiving such a sinner as he. He then relaxed his neck, shut his eyes, and stated he was ready to go home.

Father Mike and the chaplain, who had been standing in a corner of the room, walked over next to the warden who said he had seen many prisoners die before, but none as memorable to him as Nikolai. He noticed satanic tattoos covered the inmate's forearms. They were black and red, and fiercely evil looking in his eyes. He noticed the numbers 666 tattooed across the knuckles on both of Nikolai's hands.

This particular prisoner had once shaved his long, dark, greasy hair into two tufts on the top of his head that resembled horns. Then, after giving his life to the Lord, he tried letting it grow out, but it didn't get very long after only three months. Also, while Nikolai had been praying, the warden noticed that he had once chiseled two of his incisor teeth into fangs. The man was confused as to why an obvious devil worshipper was praying to God. What he didn't know was that if Nikolai could have changed the shape of his teeth, he would have.

Father Mike patted Nikolai kindly on the shoulder, causing him to open his eyes again. Looking over, he noticed the look of disapproval on the warden's face, but it didn't matter to him anymore. He was ready to get this over with, and no longer worry about what people were thinking of him. Lifting his neck, Nikolai noticed the warden nod his head to the anteroom, indicating to the multiple executioners hidden from view to begin administering the lethal drugs.

Putting his head back down, Nikolai turned his neck toward the witness room and mouthed the words, "I'm sorry," over and over. Neither he, nor the witnesses, could see each one of the executioners injecting drugs into the IV tubes going into Nikolai's arms—this is done so that only one of the executioners is actually delivering the lethal injection, and none of them knows who has delivered the lethal dose and who has injected drugs into a dummy bag.

After five grams of Pentothal, a general anesthetic, was injected, Nikolai fell into a deep sleep so he wouldn't feel anything thereafter. Upon seeing this, Father Mike sighed, grateful that he had the privilege of witnessing this man change the course of his life. Next, Pavulon, a muscle relaxant, was given in a dose that stopped Nikolai's breathing by paralyzing his diaphragm and lungs.

Finally, he was injected with a lethal dose of Potassium Chloride, the final drug that induced the cardiac arrest that the EKG machine detected. A member of the team entered the chamber from the anteroom and declared Nikolai dead. The warden scoffed, causing the chaplain to look at him with noticeable disgust. After all, this person was someone's son, possibly someone's brother, or perhaps somebody's uncle, husband, or father.

After thirty minutes went by, the guards returned from the anteroom to place Nikolai in a body bag and then they took him to the medical examiner. Both guards grimaced a bit; it wasn't enjoyable for them to watch a man die. Nonetheless, it was their job to wait until the prisoner was confirmed deceased so they could remove his body from the execution chamber.

They weren't privy to it, but Nikolai was already absent from his body and standing before the mighty *judgment seat* of the Lord (not to be confused with the *great white throne* where those who aren't going to Heaven have their judgment). Because he went straight to Heaven, Nikolai didn't visit the *holding area,* the *room of gifts,* or the *room of files.*

Scouring the area in a hopeful manner, Nikolai saw that he was no longer in the execution room of the prison, but standing outside a magnificent looking palace. Relieved and joyful, he began skipping around like a giddy boy, free of earthly shame. His childlike faith had paid off—this wasn't the Hell described in the Bible, so Nikolai believed he must be in Heaven. *It was all true! What the Bible said of life and death was all true,* Nikolai thought. Even though he was a grown man, he jumped up and down with delight—thankful that he had prayed the prayer of salvation, and even more grateful that the God of Heaven by all accounts was real.

The angelic emissary, who had escorted him from Earth, patted Nikolai on the back. He could see how happy the new arrival was to be in paradise. To Nikolai, it looked like they were standing in some sort of courtyard or park. Surveying the area, he noticed shade trees, soft luscious grass, and benches. He then looked down and was shocked to see that he was walking on cobblestones made of gold. The angel chuckled after seeing Nikolai gasp. Heaven's newest arrival thought the area reminded him of the community park outside of the city hall in the small town he grew up in, except for the gold stones, of course.

"Follow me," said the celestial being, smiling with delight. He took Nikolai into the area of Heaven called the *judgment seat*. Upon walking in, Nikolai was amazed at how sacred and consecrated the foyer seemed. The messenger of God then took the new arrival's arm and led him into the courtroom-type area.

"Nikolai Von Kozlowski," the Holy Spirit called. He jumped back at the sheer sound of his name echoing through the grandiose palace. For the first time since his arrival in Heaven, he remembered his former life. Nikolai's head slumped and his hands wrung. He wanted to look up and around and take in the sheer beauty of the throne room in all its magnificence, but he felt humbled, and surrendered like never before in his life.

Keeping his eyes lowered in a manner of subordination, he finally conjured the courage to look up. Nikolai Kozlowski almost fainted when he saw the awesome God of the Universe seated on His royal throne. He gasped at the royalty, righteousness, and purity of the towering figure. Just as the lion is the king of beasts on Earth, he was certain this lion was the King of Heaven. He had a presence about Him that radiated honor and respect.

"Nikolai, my son," the royal-looking, majestic lion with a golden mane and stunningly blue eyes said in a language that was recognizable to Heaven's newest tenant.

"You are standing before me, your God, because you had the courage to believe Me when I said I was the way, the truth, and the life. You had the faith of a mustard seed when you prayed with the priest. I watched with pride and joy while you accepted my heavenly invitation. You followed my instructions to be a light in the darkness—well done, my son."

Still in awe, Nikolai could barely contain himself. He got down on his knees, placing his elbows and head down, and then placed his hands up in reverence.

"Father God, I am not worthy to receive you," Nikolai humbly responded, still afraid to look up and peer into the compassionate face of the sovereign God he just met in person. "I haven't taken my life seriously, Father God. I've hurt and killed people. I've…"

"Beloved," Yahweh gently interjected, "I don't remember any of it. Your sins have been forgotten—my Son's blood wiped each of your transgressions clean the day you prayed with the priest. When you accepted my free gift of liberation, you became a brand new person. For that reason, you come before Me, clean and free from transgression."

Nikolai stood, feeling literally brand new. Because of God's unending mercy and grace, he had been found innocent. Looking down, he saw that his skin was fresh and clean; he was free of the grossly demonic tattoos. Putting his hands on his head, he noticed the two tufts of hair resembling horns were gone. He then felt his mouth and learned the two teeth he had chiseled into fangs were now smooth. Finally, Nikolai was free from the consequences of his earthly choices.

He sighed in relief, feeling his brand new body melting with contentment. All his fears, anxieties, and insecurities had melted away; he felt such gratitude to the Lord. Now that he was on the other side, he realized the benevolent nature of God was far beyond earthly understanding or comprehension.

"I want you to know that because of my love for you, I placed urgency upon your parents, friends, and family members three months ago to pray for you at the exact time you were making a decision for, or against, me. Nikolai, their prayers interceded and the Holy Spirit convicted you. You made the most important decision of your life when you chose to submit your life to me, and this is your reward for accepting the truth before it was too late," Jehovah God said, gesturing toward the gates of Heaven.

Nikolai smiled while thinking of his parents, and then he asked, "Yahweh, you are so kind and giving. Is there any way you could do me a favor before I go through?"

"Of course, my son," He replied. "What is it?"

"Is there any way you could make sure my folks are aware that I made the decision to follow you? They deserve to know where I am."

"It's already been done, my child," Almighty Father declared. Nikolai was surprised at God's response. "Nikolai, after your conversion, the priest had you write a letter to your parents asking them to forgive you for the pain and grief you caused them. Do you remember?"

"Yes. I owed them that much," Nikolai recalled.

"Son, because they could not afford to attend your execution today, they are holding a candlelight vigil on your behalf. At this very moment, your parents and family members in your home country are meeting in your small childhood church. Your father is reading the letter you wrote to them aloud. Your mother is crying with thanksgiving and joy. Your faith has touched the hearts of all the people in attendance," the Lord told Nikolai with a twinkle in His eye.

Nikolai smiled broadly, feeling proud of whom he was for the first time since he was a young boy walking the country roads of Poland.

If you recall, people in the *holding area* were watching Nikolai enter Heaven's gates, trying to guess what kind of life he had led on Earth. As they continued to watch, they witnessed divinely mystical angels escort Nikolai, along with a woman who had also just arrived, through the golden arched gates of Heaven. It was Emma La'Mone. Do you remember her? She was the woman married to the hockey star, Dominic La'Mone. She had the horrible nightmare about Hell; then she made the conversion that resulted in the biggest gift God could ever give her.

You might recall that there were many hugs and shouts from family members and friends when Emma entered the gates. Few people Nikolai knew awaited his arrival, but he didn't even notice. He now had a new family. Every soul in Heaven was his brother and sister; he would never feel isolated, lonely, or unaccepted again.

After the great reunion, Nikolai and Emma joined all of Heaven's residents for a magnificent banquet—a feast of every food imaginable. Seeing the assorted delicacies spread before him, and smelling the various aromas, made Nikolai salivate with anticipation. There were fruits and vegetables of every color and kind, a grand display of skillfully carved meats, eggs, cheeses, and potatoes...every food under the sun, and more!

The generous sustainer, God, sat at the head of the enormous table enjoying the edible aromas in the air, as well as time spent among friends. Nikolai made his way around the table until he found his name written in elegant calligraphy on a place card in front of his place setting. He marveled that his seat had been custom made for his size and particular design tastes. Sitting down, his body sank into the plush comfort of the luxurious, brown, leather chair.

Looking around, the gentle giant noted that the table was set with crisp, fine, white linens. He noticed a solid gold charger sitting beneath a white china plate, trimmed with gold and purple, etched and embossed designs. Nikolai smiled broadly when he saw an ichthus, a symbol of Christianity, inlaid in the center of his plate in the deep purple gemstone, tanzanite. He had seen the popular fish design on people's car bumpers back on Earth when he moved to America at the age of eighteen.

To the left of his plate sat a delicate crystal goblet containing his favorite beverage, as well as a solid gold goblet with the most succulent wine available. Across the table, Emma lifted her wine goblet high to offer Nikolai a toast, when his elbow accidentally spilled his goblet of red wine across the formal, white tablecloth. Jesus and the children on his lap simply laughed, while Nikolai held his breath and closed his eyes, waiting for someone to chastise him for his clumsiness.

Instead, Jesus magically made the crimson stain white as snow. When Nikolai reluctantly opened his eyelids, he exhaled in relief, and stared in awe at the transformed linen. Smiling, he marveled at how different Heaven was from Earth, and how grateful he was that God wasn't expecting robotic perfection from His special forever guests, but light-hearted celebration instead.

People all around him laughed, shared stories, and got to know each other while polished, sterling silver flatware clinked against plates, and guests passed food around from trays sitting in the middle of the elegant table. The long, narrow, alabaster trays ran the entire length of the enormous dining table and were decorated with pearls, and other sparkling jewels, as well as lit candles and fragrant flowers. Each contained an array of foods cooked to perfection, exquisite delicacies, and delectable desserts fit for a king.

Each guest dined in pure unadulterated peace, their new bodies devoid of memories of their earthly lives that could have caused sadness, negativity, or regret. Instead, they lived in the moment, knowing the joyous experience would never end.

A starry curtain served as a backdrop; the diners watched in wonder while the Lord amazingly called each star by its given name. Horns, flutes, zithers, lyres, harps, pipes, and other musical instruments played, as Heaven's armies of angels lovingly served the masses while singing in effortless harmony.

Nikolai's new and everlasting home was replete with thanksgiving and wholehearted joy. He was overwhelmed with awe and deep appreciation for the infinite and everlasting peace he now knew.

After greeting everyone and enjoying her supper, Emma knelt before the Lord and said, "Thank you, God, for second chances! Thank you for your loving kindness! Thank you for loving me the way no other could!" Nikolai threw himself down next to her. He lay prostrate, echoing her praises.

The all-sufficient One, El Shaddai, in all His glory, winked at the two of them and said, "You are welcome dear ones! Welcome home my precious children! Welcome home!"

Chapter 14
Judgment Day

Once again, the glass doors in the *holding area* lifted up. Section 8:06 a.m. had reached the end of the line. Angels once again called individual names. The souls left the *holding area* for the last time and followed the angels, one at a time, to the *great white throne*.

Teresa's heart softened when she saw the God of Heaven and Earth for herself while she had gazed out the glass panes in the *holding area*. Her heart was far more tenderer toward Him now that she had been through the *room of gifts* and the *room of files*. The two mighty and powerful angels, who had been escorting her, now motioned for her to open the next door.

A sign on the door read *great white throne*, which made Teresa uneasy. It seemed to her that God might be on the other side, and even though she had longed to meet him earlier when she was in the *holding area*, she now felt nervous about coming face to face with Him. Hence, she hesitated to reach out for the curved, iron door handle when one of the angels motioned toward it. Seeing her trepidation, the angels kindly opened it for her. She tried peeking inside before entering, but her body followed through before she was ready to face the room's contents.

The giant bronze door she crossed through must have been fifteen feet tall. Ornate iron designs covered its exterior. The room she entered looked like some sort of sacred temple. Teresa's hand instinctively rose to shield her eyes from the intensity of the light in the area, and it took a while for her pupils to refocus so that she could see. *Ai Caramba!* Teresa thought. She had never seen such a stunningly sacred palace in her lifetime.

Sheer, white linen curtains decorated the room, and there were four, grand, white, marble pillars forming a rectangular center court. Gold inlaid marble formed a center stage within the court and a dais, or raised platform, was in the middle. The platform was a gorgeous slab of white marble with flecks of different colored stones in it—they were purple, green, yellow, orange, and other bright colors. On it sat three royal-looking, high-backed chairs, each fit for a king. They were large, golden chairs with exquisitely ornate carvings on them.

A lion, representing the Almighty God of Heaven and Earth, sat in the middle chair facing her. He was majestic in appearance with a golden mane and crystal-blue eyes. In fact, Teresa thought he looked a lot like Aslan from the *Chronicles of Narnia* movie series. She remembered how she felt when she saw Aslan fight and defeat the white witch in that fabulous tale. It was a great defeat by a scary beast, but the lion sitting before her wasn't scary at all.

An unblemished white lamb sat on God's right-hand side. It was strikingly pure and innocent looking beyond reproach, reminding Teresa of a newborn baby. Yet, in reality, He was the hero—He was the Savior who gave up His life to save the world. His eyes shone with compassion and mercy while looking at His precious daughter, Teresa.

A kind-looking Spirit sat on the left of the King of Beasts. Teresa assumed, from the things her mother had told her about God and her religion, that this Spirit must be the Holy Spirit. It wasn't a scary ghost, but instead He seemed comforting and welcoming to Teresa. The Spirit appeared strong, powerful, and mighty, yet at the same time unassuming and compassionate as well. He reminded Teresa of an old, wise man that was desperately trying to extend God's love—she could see it in His soothing eyes.

Teresa also noticed what looked like a sea of crystal-clear glass in front of the dais. She could smell smoke from red, amber, and orange flames coming from sterling silver pots located on both sides of the platform. The gray smoke wafted through the air and smelled similar to incense she had smelled in the past when she visited stores in her town.

Hundreds of mighty male angels guarded the throne; the glow illuminating from them coupled with the brilliance of those on the throne lit the room. No other additional light was necessary. Light reflected off them and created a dazzling display of emerald green flickers of light behind the throne. In the center of the captivating sea of green, lightning bolts burst out in an array of majestic swirls and streaks.

Teresa slowly inched forward, further into the room, sheepishly as if she were not worthy to stand on such holy ground. For the first time in her life, stubbornness, pride, anger, bitterness, and cold-heartedness fell away from her. She stood before the trio humbled and in awe.

The Spirit spoke in an audible voice that was gentle, kind, and loving. She could tell by the compassionate intensity of the tone in His voice that He was obviously the mouthpiece of God.

"Teresa Jo Hernandez, my sweet daughter," said the voice of God ever so gently, "I created you 13,518 days ago. I made all the delicate, inner parts of your body, and knit them together in your mother's womb. I was there while you were forming in utter seclusion. I saw you before you were born, and I scheduled each day of your life before you began to breathe. Every day was recorded in my book."

Teresa recognized the Spirit's voice as the same one that came from the voice she heard in the *holding area*. Even with its unpretentious sound, the voice was all-knowing and all-powerful. She intuitively knew this was the sound of the conscience she had heard in her mind as a young girl…the voice in her head that taught her right from wrong, as well as what was good, upright, and moral.

Suddenly a video appeared in the space between her and the dais, despite the fact that Teresa saw no evidence of a projector or screen. The video played out in the air in front of her like one of those holograms in a science fiction movie, although she couldn't see from where the video originated. The image that was playing was one of her mother and father holding her as a newborn. Teresa's heart leapt when she saw the pride and adoration they shared for their baby girl.

"Teresa, I am God, your Creator, Comforter, King, Provider, and Savior—the lover of your soul. I am the great *I am*. You can see the love your earthly parents had for you, but as your heavenly Father, I love you even more."

Teresa's eyes moved to the throne and then back to the next video that caught her eye. In this video, Teresa was about four and she was sitting on a rocking chair in her mother's lap. The Bible was in Juanita's hand, and the two of them were singing together, "Yes, Jesus loves me; yes, Jesus loves me. Yes, Jesus loves me; the Bible tells me so." The tender way her mother looked at her made Teresa realize for the first time how much she had cared about her daughter's soul.

"I was there with you...that day and every day. My thoughts of you outnumbered the grains of sand on Earth. I protected you and loved you, even when your heart was cold to me," the Spirit said reminiscently.

In the next video, Teresa looked to be nine years old. She was hiding in the closet from her father, who was on a drunken rampage.

"Do you remember being in that closet, Teresa?" God asked.

"Yes, I hid there every time I was scared," she replied in a whisper.

"You didn't know it then, but I was with you every time you were in there—you were sitting on my lap, and I was holding you tight. I comforted you and made you feel peaceful until you fell fast to sleep. I never took my eyes off you all the days of your life."

Teresa thought back and could almost feel the embrace God spoke of. She recalled many days and nights in that dark and dingy closet, feeling scared and lonely. Now, tears filled her eyes; she thought of the compassion God had for her, and she wished she had realized it earlier.

The next video made Teresa jump back; she saw her husband slapping and punching her while she pleaded for him to stop. Something else caught her eye; there was a shadow behind Roberto—she didn't know it then, but God proceeded to tell her that He had been holding her husband back from causing Teresa further harm that evening.

"I was there, too, Teresa. Roberto was going to kill you that night. He was reaching for a knife, and I stopped him by substantially blurring his already impaired vision from the large amount of alcohol he had consumed. I wanted to make sure you had every day on Earth that I had planned out for you, so you would have time to get to know me and form a relationship with me. I wanted you to accept me."

"I don't understand, God. If you were there with us, then why didn't you prevent Roberto from hurting the girls and me all those times? You had the power to stop or prevent all the beatings, too. So, why didn't you?" Teresa asked with a hint of irritation in her voice.

God wasn't angry at Teresa's questions. He nodded his head in agreement that He felt she had a right to answers.

"Teresa, you learned in the *room of gifts* that I thoroughly relish opening the windows of Heaven and pouring out blessings so great that you don't have room enough to take them all in. Unfortunately, Dear One, human beings often jump the gun; they don't always include me in their decisions. Thus, sometimes they don't marry the person that was best for them, occasionally they don't choose the house I planned for them to enjoy, or some settle for a job that pays the bills but doesn't fulfill their heart's desires.

"When you don't ask for, or accept, direction from Me, you usually settle for what is good and nice, but not what was the best for you: The spouse I intended for you, the job that was perfectly designed for you, or the house best suited to your needs are just a few examples."

Teresa broke down and began to sob. She could see what God was saying. He prevented her death the night Roberto was drunk, but she had to sleep in the proverbial bed she had made…she had to live with her good *and* her bad choices. Nonetheless, even though life with Roberto had been terrible those last years, she was grateful that the two of them created their beautiful Angelica and Lupita together. If nothing else, being married to him was worth it to Teresa in consideration of the time she had with her precious daughters.

Contemplating what she was currently experiencing, she found it reassuring that the God of the Universe had taken the time to explain these things to her, rather than becoming angry and aggressive toward her. However, she was still feeling a little heated, and didn't like being in the defendant's seat, so to speak.

Looking up, Teresa saw the Lamb of God leaving the throne and heading toward the rectangular court. A spectacular gold display case stood in the center of the room. The case was very similar to the one in the *room of gifts*. Instead of the glass containing a crown, though, it held a thick book. It appeared quite old to Teresa, although she noticed it was immaculately kept.

The Lamb, in all His splendor, morphed right before her eyes into a human being that looked just like the pictures Juanita used to show Teresa of Jesus. He had shoulder-length, brown hair, a mustache, warm, gentle looking eyes, and He was wearing a long, magnificently pure white robe. Christ opened one end of the glass case, then took the thick book out and began browsing through it.

Just then, Teresa heard a hissing sound. She had been so fascinated with the mightiness of the Lord, and enthralled with His throne, that she was aghast when she saw a dark corner on the other side of the room she hadn't noticed before. Squinting her eyes, she saw a creature with seven extremely long necks that eased out of the darkness and slowly crawled toward her. On the end of each neck was the head of a repugnant snake. For the first time since she had entered the holy room, Teresa felt scared. When it was two yards from her, one of the heads stretched out its neck, nearly touching her face, just like in a 3-D movie. It hissed the words "She's mine!" in a deep, raspy, threatening tone.

Although He was the sacrificial lamb, Jesus was in no way weak; therefore, He ignored the viper's words and continued looking through the pages of the fascinating book.

The Holy Spirit spoke again, saying, "Teresa, I am interested in every aspect of your life—how you used the abilities and gifts I gave you, and how you handled relationships and opportunities granted to you. But most importantly, I want to know what you have done with my son."

Trying to ignore the viper standing far too close to her, Teresa turned her attention to the Spirit. Confused, she asked, "I don't understand the question. What do you mean? What son?"

God continued speaking through the Spirit, explaining, "My Son, Jesus, paid the penalty for your sins with His blood. I sent Him to die on the cross as your Savior, and then rise from the dead. Did you reject Him, ignore Him, or dislike Him? Were you too busy for Him? Did you feel unworthy of Him, or did you accept Him?"

"Sir," Teresa said, "I made a mistake. I didn't realize how important Jesus was. I thought he was a good man—a good teacher, or possibly a prophet. Everyone had such different beliefs on Earth; it was confusing to me. I couldn't just pick one religion to put my faith in."

"Dear, Teresa, Christ isn't a religion. I placed a desire for Him in every soul I created; yet you had more allegiance to the Dalai Lama than you had to Him. You spent time rubbing crystals and seeking psychics. You dabbled in the occult and put your faith in your horoscope rather than the Word I left behind for you. Yet, when your mother presented the Truth to you, you rejected us," the Holy Spirit said sadly.

Teresa sighed. She had no rebuttal. She had no excuses.

"Teresa, Jesus is currently looking through the *book of life*," the Spirit told her. "All of mankind's names are in it, and the names of those souls who have rejected us have been erased."

Jesus then hung His head and nodded to the lion in disappointment. Both became visibly upset and began to weep.

"Unfortunately, Satan is right, Teresa. Your name is not in the book. If it had been, you would have been an heir to the Kingdom. I wanted you to live with us here for eternity, my precious princess. I wanted you to never experience pain, sadness, or evil again, but I couldn't force you to love me, or accept my son's payment for your sins. I wanted Earth to be the only Hell you ever knew, but, by your choices, you have condemned yourself."

Hell? Teresa thought. *This can't be happening!* Her eyes scoured the area for exit doors. She was frightened and wanted to bolt from the area, but large, heavenly bodyguards were policing every exit. Sobs began to rack her body as she began to shake with fear seeing the serpent out of her peripheral vision. Reality was setting in; Teresa began to realize she would not be joining her family in paradise after all.

"God," Teresa asked boldly, "why did you send me through the *holding area* and the different rooms when it appears I'm not going to Heaven? Are you sadistic, or do you just enjoy prolonging the torment and torture of people like me?" Now that Teresa had nothing to lose, she let loose of her aggressive hostility with both barrels. Since this was her last chance to state her defense, she decided to demand more explanation.

"Teresa, think of this analogy: Teachers don't *give* their students grades; students *earn* their grades. So when a student is mad at a teacher for receiving a C in math, he or she must be reminded that the teacher was in the position of helping the student succeed, not fail. Likewise, I want every person I create to live with me for eternity; if a person decides to decline the invitation, I want to show that person how I tried to help them succeed.

"In this example, the teacher would have shown the student that they didn't turn in their homework, they did poorly on tests, or they missed too many days of school, so they would see why their grade wasn't what they had hoped it would be. Similarly, by going through the different rooms plus the *great white throne*, I gave you a chance to realize that I was not picking on you, that I had not forgotten or neglected you, or set you up for a fall. Instead, you were given the opportunity to see how your own choices determined your fate."

Realizing the supreme judge had evaluated her secrets, plus her innermost thoughts and motives, and found her guilty, Teresa cried out, "How about if we make a deal?" Seeing the serpent slithering toward her, Teresa shouted, while backing away, "Please make sure that my daughter, Lupita, knows the truth. And, please remember that I did do some really nice things, you know. I was a good person most of the time…"

"Away from me, you evildoer," the Spirit commanded sadly. "I never knew you," He said with deep regret.

Now it was Teresa's turn to accept the consequences of her decisions. She watched in horror as the seven-headed snake morphed into a large furry, black beast. She thought it looked almost like a buffalo—it was covered in black fur and it stood on two legs. Ten massive horns were on its head, and its eyes blazed with red and yellow fire. Teresa tried to drag her broken limbs away from the creature, but, before she knew it, he had her in his clutches. As the beast led her from the room, she screamed, "I'm sorry. Let me stay...let me..."

It was finished. Teresa Jo Hernandez was led away from the Lord God's presence for all eternity.

Chapter 15
Last Embrace

The overhead lights were bright in the ICU of the hospital, and the noise level was quite loud when the doctors removed the paddles from Lupita's chest. While she had been in a coma, her heart had stopped. No one in the room knew Lupita had just had a near-death experience, and had spent time in section 9:02 p.m. of the *holding area* where she spoke with the voice of God.

The doctors had been trying to resuscitate her for nearly twelve minutes when, with the final shock of the defibrillator, she began showing signs of life. Because she had arrived at the hospital from the scene of the accident the morning before with no living relatives for the doctors to confer with, they weren't aware of her medical history. No one from her past could share with them the fact that she had congenital heart disease. Her parents learned of it when she was born, but it hadn't caused her problems in the past. Accordingly, everyone just crossed his or her fingers hoping that she would eventually outgrow it.

Now that she was showing a normal cardiac rhythm, she seemed to be out of the woods. She was receiving IV fluids, while doctors and nurses frantically watched her vital signs for indications of improvement.

By now, it was 9:32 p.m. and Lupita lay quietly sleeping in the ICU. No one in the room knew the young girl had lost all desire to live. It was their job to keep her alive, yet Lupita was ready to die. Within an hour, her vital signs started to worsen, and her organs began to shut down. Onlooking doctors were astounded that such a vibrant teenager was no longer fighting for her life. They didn't want to admit it, but, in the back of their minds, they realized Lupita was slipping away quickly.

At 11:35 p.m., the lone nurse who was watching Lupita noticed an unusually broad smile appear on her patient's face. Lupita's eyes fluttered a bit, while tears of joy gently rolled down her cheeks. One of the doctors who had been attending to Lupita earlier happened to be walking in the ICU corridor, so the nurse ran out and grabbed his arm, asking him to check on her patient's rapidly declining condition.

Without warning, both were shocked to see the monitor next to her bed flat line. Working together, they tried over and over to resuscitate Lupita. Yet this time, it was to no avail. The teenager's death was disappointing to the two caregivers who realized that they had just witnessed the pretty, sixteen-year-old take her last breath. The nurse noted on her chart, time of death: March 3 at 11:58 p.m.

If only the medical staff could have seen what was happening in that room the moment Lupita's heart stopped once and for all. The sweet angel of death had arrived to take Pita home for good. Opening her eyes to the afterlife, she startled in amazement at his radiant beauty. The medical personnel couldn't see it, but the room immediately filled with an explosion of light at his presence. To Lupita, his appearance was comforting, magnetizing, and exhilarating. Wrapping her hand in his, she felt no fear or compulsion to stay in the dreary room that reeked of death while he beckoned her to follow him to the pathway leading to eternal life. The angel's face filled with joy, as if he were ecstatic to be the one escorting Pita to her new heavenly residence.

Lupita, too, was excited. Since she had glimpsed at the Holy City earlier, she no longer desired life on Earth. There was no pleasure for her in the fallen world around her; thus, she anticipated her eternal life with every part of her, down to the core of her very being.

Within an instant, the two of them were on their way home. They moved upwards toward the sky above the hospital. In the back of her mind, Lupita understood that they were walking through walls, and even through the roof, while departing the hospital. The human part of her wanted to worry that she might bump into the walls and ceilings even as she passed through them, but her soul knew better.

Lupita was enthralled at the idea of living in the paradise she had witnessed earlier. She could hardly wait to see the innocent, everloving face of her sovereign Father God again. Lupita held on tight to her guardian angel while they dipped and dived up, up, up, through the atmosphere. Once they arrived in the hereafter, the angel gingerly placed her feet on holy ground, and then shared a secret with her.

"Lupita," he said looking into her eyes, "I am a messenger of the Lord. Because He is filled with compassion for his children, God is granting you a special treat—one that few receive. Lupita, you must walk down this cobblestone path until you reach a golden bench with a red rose lying across it. Sit there until I return."

Teresa did exactly as the angel had directed, all the while wondering what the special treat could be. Still curious about the turn of events, she noticed there were several golden benches in an area located between the *great white throne* and the *judgment seat,* so Lupita found the one with the rose on it, and sat down.

While sitting and waiting, she took in every ounce of the beauty of Heaven: the fluffy white clouds that looked like cotton balls, tall flowering trees with the sounds of chirping birds coming from them, the smells of the numerous colorful flowers—lily of the valley...rose of Sharon—and the beauty of several effortlessly fluttering hummingbirds.

Looking further, she was surprised to see there were no brown or yellow patches in the grass; there were no weeds, sticker patches, dandelions, or tumbleweeds. *Ai yai yai! This is definitely Heaven,* she thought, beaming at the radiance all around her. Upon further reflection, Lupita noticed it wasn't a windy day, nor was it bitter cold, or scorchingly hot either, like many days she remembered on Earth. She knew she had entered an unparalleled paradise.

Curious, she looked down around the foot of the bench. Lupita also noticed there were no crawling critters such as annoying ants, scary spiders, or creepy bugs...this was definitely her own special nirvana. Giddy, Lupita smiled and sighed while she picked up the delicate, scarlet rose lying next to her. *My goodness,* she thought, *it doesn't even have thorns!*

Meanwhile, in an unusual state of events, the angel met up with Satan, who had Teresa in his clutches after removing her from the *great white throne*. Of course, the devil put up a fight, but he was no match for the warrior angel, and he knew it.

"Lucifer," the mighty angel said, "the Lord God has commanded me to take this woman for one last visit with her daughter. I will return her to you soon. Until then, I demand that you release her into my custody."

Satan was completely aware that he was subordinate to the King of Kings and His mighty army of angels; therefore, he released Teresa as ordered.

"Don't forget, she's mine!" he growled.

Teresa was shocked at the turn of events. *Did the angel really say what I thought he said?* She went from being led to Hell, to being led to see her baby girl—*Could this really be happening?* she wondered in anticipation.

She couldn't have been more elated! "My daughter? Are you saying I will see Angelica again?" Teresa asked the mesmerizing angel-man.

"No, Teresa. Your daughter, Lupita, succumbed to her injuries caused by the accident."

Teresa looked fearfully at the angel, so he continued. "She searched her soul during her last two days on Earth, and chose to welcome Jesus into her heart."

The proud mother couldn't help but smile, knowing Pita would join her sister and the others in Heaven.

"Teresa, God is granting her one last visit with you. Follow me, please."

The angel led Teresa to the bench Lupita was waiting on. When Lupita turned and saw her mother limping down the path toward her, she was up and in her mother's embrace in a heartbeat. In her wildest dreams, she would have never guessed the *treat* the angel spoke of was seeing her mother again. The two held each other for a very long time, happy that the loving God of Heaven had been so kind to them.

The angel left them alone. Tears streamed down mother and daughter's faces as they embraced. Teresa then took Lupita's face in her hands. She wanted to memorize every strand of hair, every freckle, every tint of her beautiful daughter's eyes, so that she could dream of her lovely beauty forever and ever.

"Mija, I have always loved you. Never ever forget that!" Teresa told her eldest daughter.

Sitting down on the bench next to each other, Lupita laid her head on her madre's shoulder, while the two of them shared memories. Teresa told Lupita about the day she was born, and how Roberto barely got her to the hospital in time due to a flat tire on the way. She reminded Lupita how she had been named after Roberto's mother.

Teresa then reminded Lupita of the first day of kindergarten, when a little boy spilled milk all over the five-year-old's pretty, new, red dress. Lupita laughed when she recalled that experience. She remembered punching that boy and hearing him scream like a girl. She giggled at the memory.

They had a very special time of reminiscing, until the angel returned. Neither woman wanted the moment to come in which they would have to part. Each knew in their hearts that they would be separated forevermore. It was a touching moment that even the angel didn't want to interrupt.

When he began to gently lead Teresa's broken body away, Lupita lunged forward to break his grasp from her mother, but Teresa pushed her away and told her precious daughter to go and receive the rewards she deserved. Lupita wanted to cling to her mother, yet deep down inside, Heaven felt like a magnet to her. It was pulling her; she was being beckoned to her rightful home, while the angel ever so lovingly and tenderly led her mother in the opposite direction.

Looking back, Teresa marveled at the exquisite beauty of her lovely Pita, who looked so grown up and mature as she walked the golden cobblestones of Heaven. Her flowing white robes and long dark curls were long out of sight, yet Teresa continued looking back, practically breaking her neck to witness the purity of her precious daughter, while the angel lovingly coaxed her in the opposite direction. She couldn't stop the tears from flowing down her cheeks as pride intermixed with sadness and fear left Teresa wondering what would happen next.

The angel led Teresa back to where the souls from section 8:06 a.m. were waiting. Feeling fear and regret, it felt like her legs were as heavy as cement as she dreaded joining Anthony, Vickie, and the others outside the *great white throne* again. All the while, the words she heard earlier from God echoed in her mind: "I wanted Earth to be the only Hell you ever knew, but, by your choices, you have condemned yourself."

Crying loudly as she walked along, Teresa noticed Vickie trembling next to her, and then it seemed everyone in the group screamed as the beast, Satan, transformed before their eyes into a large, ferocious, red dragon with spikes running down its back. It bellowed and blew flames of fire at the crowd to further scare them.

Teresa felt the heat from the monster's breath, and noticed the stench of sulfur filling the air as the hideously repulsive creature then danced with delight; he was reciting the many ways he had tricked, lied to, and brainwashed his new tenants. Many had been wooed by money, success, material possessions, and power—all that was left behind on Earth when they died.

While walking next to Teresa, Anthony screamed when something poked him in the back. He turned around at the same time Teresa did; they saw hundreds of eerie black demonic spirits with piercing fingers that looked like pitchforks herding them along with the other captives. Their eyes grew big and they became even more fearful and scared.

The evil demon beings shrieked like laughing hyenas as they pushed and shoved Teresa and the other unwilling dead souls away from the outside of the *holding area's* view of the eternal joys of Heaven. It was becoming clearer and clearer to Teresa where she and the others were headed.

Shockingly, each step Satan's prisoners took brought forth the pain and suffering each person should have been feeling since their earthly deaths. For instance, Teresa and Herb immediately felt their broken bones, bruises, and cuts caused by the accidents that killed them. Unfortunately, there was no medicine, casts, or salve to apply that would alleviate the tortuous aching.

Vickie felt sick to her stomach from overdosing; she needed her stomach pumped, yet was forced to endure the unending distress during the long walk. Anthony almost passed out once he saw the amount of blood leaving his body from the knife wound that landed him in a body bag. The tormenting anguish from the sharp pains to his abdominal area caused him extreme anxiety and gnashing of teeth.

People such as Maxine and Reuben, who hadn't died painful deaths, now felt the suffering of eternal separation from God the Father. They screamed and cried out in desperation, pleading for the mercy and grace they had shunned their entire lives. Although it was too late, Teresa and the others finally understood and appreciated the truth about the saving power of Almighty God. Teresa's mind recalled a bumper sticker she had seen on the back of someone's car that stated, *Not of this world.* She had never understood its meaning until this very moment.

Her story was coming to a tragic end, while Angelica and Lupita's were just beginning.

Chapter 16
New Beginning

After her precious visit with her mother, a sweet angel escorted Lupita to the *judgment seat*. Because she was going to Heaven, she didn't experience the *room of files* or *room of gifts* that Teresa had. Ordinarily, she would have never stepped foot in the *holding area* either, except that God, in His tender mercy, gave her a near-death experience so that she would be thoughtful about the decision she was making for, or against, Him.

Arriving at the *judgment seat* was the pinnacle of Lupita's life. She could hardly wait to see His Highness on His throne. The thought of her daddy being the Ruler of Heaven and Earth made Pita feel safe and secure. Being his forever daughter was not only comforting to Lupita, but the idea made her skip around, hooting and hollering like she had won the prize of a lifetime.

Once inside, like those before her, Lupita was in awe at the breathtaking throne of God. The throne resembled the *great white throne* her mother had told her she encountered, except there were no guards at the doors. Thankfully, her experience was not going to be a terrifying time of judgment of sins as it had been for Teresa, but, rather, a reflection of her short life.

When Jesus opened the *books of remembrance*, Lupita's life was laid out before her. Every good deed and good thought was listed. Teresa received rewards for them, plus rewards for what she had done on Earth that withstood the test of fire. Every time she had cursed, judged someone unfairly, lied, or was lead by selfish ambition, conceit, personal gain, and other worthless endeavors were listed as well. Consequently, she lost rewards for these things she did that burned up.

The greatest reward she received, of course, was salvation—being an heir to Heaven forevermore. Other rewards included never being afraid of the dark again, never experiencing any form of evil again, and never being afraid or fearful again. As a citizen of the Holy City, she would never experience hatred, divorce, murder, adultery, thievery, lies, gossip, or any kind of life-altering trauma again. Instead, what lie ahead was never-ending pleasure…everlasting utopia.

When Jesus, the Lamb, opened the *book of life* to find Lupita's name, the serpent slithered forth and hissed, "She's mine!" as he had done with Teresa and every soul who came before God, but, this time, Jesus corrected him by saying, "No, Lucifer, her name is in the book. By the power of the resurrection, my blood covers her sins." Eternally defeated, the devil seethed, as the Lamb looked at Lupita and said, "Well done my good and faithful servant. You are an heir to my Kingdom!"

He stood with his arms outstretched to her, and Lupita ran to the sacred throne and jumped into the lap of the King of Kings. She held his neck tightly, never wanting to let go. Time stood still as she recalled the many questions she had for him and she was ecstatic at the chance to ask them face to face.

He lovingly stroked her long, dark hair, and listened intently while she looked into His loving eyes, and asked, "Why did you allow my brother, Timmy, to die of sudden infant death syndrome? Why do bad things happen to good people? Why hasn't a cure for cancer been found? Is there life on other planets?"

God patiently answered her numerous questions, while Pita reveled in spending special time alone with Him. Eventually God revealed all the secrets of the universe to her.

Afterward, angels escorted her through the *tunnel of treasures* where she received her *crown of life*—this was her ticket to the Kingdom of Heaven. Her headdress was simply solid gold, making her feel like the daughter of the King. She was now a royal princess with all the privileges that came with being the Supreme Ruler's daughter.

Each person who traveled through the *tunnel of treasures* received their crown, bejeweled according to the choices they made during his or her earthly lives. Accordingly, some crowns included jewels, such as rubies, topaz, onyx, and sapphires, based on what they had been given and what they had achieved for His glory. Being always fair and just, God looked deeply at each soul's heart, at his or her earthly motives, and at what kind of steward each had been with His Son.

Lupita, filled with enchantment, felt giddy again while skipping along in her treasured tiara, free from the aches, pains, worries, fears, and stresses of her previous life. Her ever-beloved guardian angel once again appeared to escort her to the place of her dreams, her own personal promised land.

Lupita giggled with astonishment, looking ahead and seeing the gates of Heaven ajar. She felt like an elegant bride, dressed in her flowing white gown and golden headdress, while walking toward the multitudes of Heaven that were singing and dancing their way over to meet and greet her. Two other brand-new tenants, Cheng and Foday, were entering the gates along with her. On Earth, all three had been strangers to each other, but, in Heaven, they were now family members.

Lupita watched the once Asian woman named Cheng throw her arms high into the air and rush through the gates exuberantly. The astonished woman couldn't believe her eyes as she marveled at the purity awaiting her.

Cheng gasped when she looked down at her new body and saw that she was no longer old, wrinkled, and hunched over as she had been on Earth. Cheng then looked up. Her hand immediately shot to her mouth, as she gulped at seeing the glory of the Lord hovering above her. Squealing with delight to be in the presence of the King of Kings, she blew a kiss toward Him.

"Thank you, most holy God, for accepting me into eternity!" Cheng yelled gleefully up to Him.

"No, my darling, you accepted me, and we shall live together forever!" God replied tenderly.

Cheng had secretly had an abortion when she was twenty years old. She could never forgive herself for it, so she punished herself by separating from family and friends. Because her family raised her to worship a Buddha statue made of sandstone, she had never understood the mercy and tender love of a living god. She thought that being a kind, good person would lead her to true peace and tranquility. However, those emotions never surpassed the self-condemnation she judged herself with.

A lifetime later, when she lay in a hospital bed, as an old woman dying of pneumonia, a chaplain visited and asked her to pray with him. She explained that she wasn't worthy of the one true God because of her past sin. The chaplain reassured her that if she were truly remorseful, her sins would be forgiven once she confessed them.

He went on to explain God's grace to Cheng, who could hardly believe Adonai would accept her on her deathbed. The idea of being rid of the shame and guilt she had lived with for fifty-nine years overwhelmed her. She dearly wanted to be loved unconditionally by the living God, so she lovingly submitted herself and prayed to accept Christ as her redeemer.

Shortly thereafter, she died peacefully in her sleep. In the blink of an eye, her lungs were strong again, her skin was youthful, and she smiled broadly, while walking through the entrance gates of the spectacularly manicured garden, taking in the majesty of the reigning Lord.

The man walking through the gates next to Lupita was Foday. Upon passing through the gates, he broke into a dance when he saw the glorious lights of Heaven. Foday hadn't thought he could be forgiven either. He had killed a man in his tiny village when the two of them were fighting over food for their families. When Foday lost his grip on the bag they each wanted, Togar, his opponent, fell backward and hit his head on a large stone—the blow killed him instantly.

Foday was shocked and saddened at what had happened. In his mind, killing a man was too big of a sin for which to be forgiven. With that in mind, he carved many idols out of wood, metal, and stone, and offered sacrifices to them in exchange for his sins, as was the custom in his culture. Yet nothing set him free from the feelings of regret until British missionaries visited his region of Africa. They introduced him to the God of Peace and gave him a Bible converted into his own language. Once he learned he could be reconciled with God through Christ's atoning sacrifice, he wanted to pray with them and dedicate the rest of his life to Christ. He did, and here he stood reaping the eternal rewards!

Foday knelt down in front of God, raised his hands above his head, and sang, "All glory and honor to the Lord most high. Thank you, most generous Yahweh, for bringing me into your presence." His face was beaming as he smiled at his intimate and sovereign maker.

The Lord smiled down and said, "Foday, my son, you were lost and now you are found. Your new name shall be *Freedom*, for you have been liberated and set free. Enjoy your rewards while living with me for all eternity."

The saints of Heaven gathered around the new arrival as he knelt at the gates of Zion. A man stepped through the crowd and walked up to shake Foday's hand. He stared up at the man in amazement. It was Togar, the man he had killed on Earth. The two embraced—there was no animosity, anger, or even shame between them. Both were at peace knowing they were found innocent at the *judgment seat.*

While the two men reunited, the saints introduced Cheng to a beautiful dark-haired girl. She was the child Cheng had aborted on Earth. The girl was now grown and gorgeous, thankful she had been spared life on Earth...the only Hell she would have ever known. The two embraced, and God smiled, while all the saints of Heaven began to sing and dance.

Nana, Richard, and Angelica ran to greet Lupita at Heaven's gates. They were so pleased to see her—it was a delightful reunion to behold. They hugged and kissed each other without a single regret or feeling of remorse, not even over Teresa. Instead, they celebrated together while they and the other saints made a parade toward the mansions prepared for Cheng, Foday, and Lupita. Each of their new homes were customized and designed according to their individual tastes.

Holding hands, the threesome skipped and shouted, "Hallelujah," while they looked in awe at the beauty set before them. They saw the sacred mountain and the tree of life Foday had read about in his Bible. The sovereignty of the Lord shone so brightly, there was no need for a moon or sun, day or night. They saw people from the Bible, such as Noah, Adam, and Sarah. Foday could hardly wait to get settled, so he could find the apostles and the martyrs and spend time talking and sharing with them.

Lupita surveyed the area and noticed that everyone was equal in her new home. No longer were people separated according to skin color, religious views, size, or gender. Everyone spoke the same language—there was no favoritism or racism. No one was shunned or made to feel inferior. She was finally home.

Gazing up, she saw the all-knowing, everpresent, all-powerful, living, loving God she had given control of her life to smiling back at her. He looked down at all of His children with adoration, much like a new parent stares at his newborn child for hours on end, only with infinite patience and perfect love.

No words could describe what Lupita was experiencing—eternity in paradise—life to the fullest with the Alpha and the Omega!

"My beloved, Pita," the Lord Jehovah called out joyfully down to her, "you have a new identity and you are receiving a new beginning, while you experience life to the fullest here in paradise! Enjoy your rewards, precious one, enjoy!"

If this book has touched your heart, or made you less fearful of death and more confident of your destiny, pass it along to someone else who will benefit from it. Or, better yet, order copies for your loved ones and friends at amazon.com. To receive a special discount from me, go to christikari.com.

Blessings, *Christi*

Acknowledgements

I am grateful to the following people who made this idea for a book come to fruition:

My family;
American Book Publishing;
My editor, Jennifer Powell;
My publisher, Gail Woodward-Wright;
My friends: Connie, Claudia, Kristen, Pattie, Ylia, Irene, Janet, and William;
My church, High Desert Church in Victorville, CA;
My God.

About the Author

Christi Kari studied communications at Fort Hays State University in Hays, Kansas, where she realized her passion for writing and designing. Over the years, she has written different types of non-fiction pieces for her places of work, her church, and other organizations. *On the Other Side of the Glass* is her first work of fiction.

Mrs. Kari resides in sunny Southern California, with her husband, Shawn, and their two children, Alexis and Jesse.